Women of Jericho Series

Return to Jericho

I0658090

Vickie L. Mosley

HerBet Publishing

Printed in the United States of America

All Contents: Written by the Author
Published By: HerBet Publishing
Editing: Wendy Bray
Book Cover Design: HerBet Publishing
Book Cover Image: Getty Images

Biblical scriptures throughout this book are found in NIV, NLB, NKJ, and the Amplified versions of the bible.

ISBN: 978-1-7327964-1-6

Dedication

To my dad and the rest of my loved ones who are now citizens of Heaven, I honor you today. You were greatly loved and are deeply missed. Take your rest and I will see you again in paradise.

Prologue

"Artie! Girl, grab a dress and your stilettos. Jesse's family, including his big brother, are in town, and he's the *sweetest* piece of eye candy you *ever* want to see," Jordin Rivers's voice broke over the phone.

"Oh Lord, girl, you are so crazy." Aleeya Thomas, rolling her eyes, laughed heartily. Good ole Jordin, the girl was always on the prowl in search of a man for her.

"I'm not playing… you better get home and fix your face so you can meet us at the restaurant by seven."

"A blind date…seriously? Jordi, you know I don't do blind dates!"

"What? Girl, you better stop playing with me. Why not? You're an attractive, single, available woman with a good job, a good head on your shoulders, and no kids."

"You sound like a used car salesman trying to sell off an old Buick or something. Anyway. I-I just plan on chilling tonight after work." Aleeya knew she wasn't being honest, but she didn't want to go there with her friend about the real reason behind her hesitation.

"Okay, correct me if I'm wrong but wasn't it you who said their biological clock was nearly broke? And if you were ever going to have a child that needed to be sooner, not later...what has changed?"

Aleeya knew what Jordin was fishing for. Yes, her on-again, off-again relationship with Paul Tate was kind of on-again. This time she was hoping that they'd be headed to the altar real soon. But Jordin thought he was like a leopard that would never change its spots. The conversation would likely go downhill from there, so she better change the subject to avoid a disagreement. "Listen, even if I wanted to go, duty calls. The Kincaid's are at it again."

"Father in heaven! Not them again?" Jordin said distastefully. "What is it this time...the kids? What, did Russell steal something? Or is Rachel having one of her infamous temper tantrums? Ooh, wait -wait, I know... it's the first of the month. So, Sherri got her welfare check which means her dead-beat husband Terry must be back in town!"

"Ladies and gentlemen, we have a winner with answer number three," Aleeya laughed as Jordin continued her rant. It felt good to know she had someone who understood the stress of counseling difficult clients.

Jordin and Aleeya had become fast friends when she signed on at the counseling agency. At first Aleeya was only hired as a temp but Jordin saw Aleeya's passion for counseling and before she knew it, the agency had hired her fulltime with Jordin being her direct supervisor.

But supervisor was one of the many roles Jordin played in Aleeya's life. The genuine friendship they had forged over the last two years was priceless. Actually, they were more like sisters than supervisor and supervisee. It was Jordin who had been so instrumental in getting her to re-commit her life to Christ six months ago. And it was Jordin who helped her realize that she should expect more from her relationship with Paul.

"You're the pearl of great price Aleeya, and if Paul can't see the true jewel, you are, then forget him. There's too many good fish in the sea for you to settle for a small crappie". If only things in life were that simple. She would throw Paul back in the sea, Sherri would throw Terry back in the cesspool he slithered out from and life would be golden. Jordin aggravated growl snapped her out of her daydream.

"Augh! This family gets on my doggone nerves... but like you said, duty calls." Jordin sighed heavily. "Give me about twenty minutes, and I'll meet you at Sherri's trailer."

"Oh no you don't!" Aleeya said firmly. "You and your hubby have been looking forward to spending some time with his family. There is no need for both of our nights to be ruined. Besides, I'm only seven minutes away, and I don't plan on staying long."

"I-I don't know Artie...I don't want you walking into a tense situation all by yourself," Jordin stated.

"Jordi... girl, please don't sweat it.... I got this! I'll be in and out before you leave your driveway. I'll be fine...you worry too much."

"Yeah... but girl, it's check day, and you know how crazy Sherri and Terry can act over money. *No*, I think I'd better just call Jess and tell him I'll be a little late."

"That makes no sense. Why should you change all your plans to come across town just to deal with this foolishness?"

"Yeah, but you never know when foolishness can turn into a crisis," Jordin cautioned.

"Okay then, if it makes you feel better, we'll do the fifteen-minute rule so you can make sure I'm safe.... but I can guarantee when you call, I'll be back in my car headed home." Aleeya assured. A sudden beeping sound in her ear caused her to look at her phone's caller ID. Recognizing the number, she paused breathed out slowly before speaking. "Jordi, I have another call I need to take, but as I said, don't bother coming. I got it covered!"

"Artie...are you sure?"

"Positive. Have fun, and I'll talk to you in about twenty minutes." Aleeya said before clicking Jordin off. Taking a second to compose herself, she clicked over to the other line.

"Hey, sexy lady!" Paul Tate's low tenor caused a quickening in her pulse and her skin to tingle with excitement. "I miss seeing your beautiful face."

"I-I miss yours too," she said softly. With a deep inhale Aleeya imagined breathing in the musky scent of his aftershave. It was always that intoxicating smell that was present right before they kissed. Biting her lips to suppress the moan in her throat. She closed her eyes momentarily knowing she should pray for God to give her strength but instead wished God would turn a blind eye to past, present, and future indiscretions she wanted to commit with this man. Shuttering with every word his soothing tenor spoke, she could feel herself rapidly falling down the rabbit hole of sin brought on by a tidal wave of hormones and lustful memories.

"Then why are you doing this to us, baby? You know in your heart that I'm your man, and you're my woman. No marriage license can change that. It definitely won't change the way we feel about each other?"

"But in God's eyes it will." The spirit of God whispered to her.

"I...", she let the rest of her words go unspoken. She was caught between the lie of the devil and the Word of Truth.

"Then why allow a piece of paper separate us? You know me, and I definitely know you, baby...don't forget that."

That was her problem, *forgetting.* She couldn't forget Paul's gorgeous face. Those piercing brown eyes that so often bore into hers. His soft full lips that housed the sexiest smile she had ever seen. Then there was that perfectly shaped bald head of his that she adored cradling as he stood over her to give her a mind-blowing kiss. All of that was wrapped in a six-foot-one athletic body coated in a dark chocolate shell. And that was just his looks she could begin to think about how good he made her feel during intimacy? Just thinking about made her crack her car window so she could get some much-needed air.

Being with him the last two years, she thought she'd died going back to that lonely existence her singlehood had shrouded her in. "Is wanting to be wanted so wrong?" Aleeya questioned as her throat began to tighten with emotion.

> *Marriage is honorable, and the wedding bed is undefiled.*

The bible verse was clear. God honored marriage. So that little piece of paper mattered to God, and the truth be told, it mattered to her too. "All of this is wrong Paul. I shouldn't have let you move in with me." Aleeya's voice cracked with the confession.

"Awe, babe, now don't go saying stuff like that. We love one another. Moving in together only strengthened our commitment," Paul interjected.

"No, marriage does that!" Aleeya thought within herself. So far, the only thing living with Paul had done was caused her relationship with God to veer off course and put her deeper in debt.

Deep down, she knew it was wrong for two professing Christians to live together before marriage, no matter how many justifiable reasons they came up with. Even when she wasn't a Christian, she told herself she'd never live with a man. "Humph, the man who wants me better come correct, meaning he better have a job and a ring." She'd tell her friends. Then, out of nowhere, Paul popped up in her life, and all of that including her good sense flew right out the window. Paul was the nicest looking man she had ever dated. But it wasn't all about his physical appeal. Paul was intelligent and ambitious too. He wanted to use his talents as a worship leader and songwriter to honor God, and he wanted her along by his side...what more could she ask for?

"*A wedding ring for starters, or for him to pay his half of the rent on time...what about him picking up after himself, and for goodness' sake, can the man keep a regular nine to five!*" Aleeya had to shake her head to get Jordi's last tirade about Paul's less than admirable ways out of her ear.

"So, babe, let's talk about our future. Why don't you grab something for dinner, and I'll meet you at the house in twenty minutes?" Paul suggested.

"Well, baby, to tell you the truth...I ahh..." She hesitated, knowing he wasn't going to like her answer. But before she could respond he abruptly interjected.

"Ahh...b-babe, ho-hold on...hold on a sec...I need to take this call." Paul clicked over before she could reply.

Looking out into the evening sky as she drove the familiar road to Sherri's trailer park, Aleeya fretted over doing the one thing she wished she wouldn't have to do...telling Paul that his moving out was permanent. There was no escaping it. If she was going to truly honor God in her personal life, she and Paul couldn't continue living together. It was marriage or bust.

Choose this day who you will serve...God or man!

The scripture verse had rung in her ears all week long with its simple message. Follow God or follow Paul? When she stacked God's faithfulness against Paul's, there was really no comparison. God won, hands down. She had been on the outs with God for far too long because of her desire to keep Paul.

"But he loves me, Lord...why must I give up his love?" Aleeya remembered crying out to the Lord one night and was surprised when first Corinthians thirteen and one immediately popped into her mind.

Love is patient...love is kind...love is not easily provoked, seeking sound wisdom.

She read quickly through it, almost quoting it by heart. But then she felt prompted to insert Paul's name for the word love and re-read the verse. "Paul is patient..." Ah no, he's not. "Paul is kind..." Not always. "Paul is not easily provoked, and he seeks sound wisdom." Ha! Okay, that definitely doesn't reflect Paul, me either, for that matter!

Then he's not a reflection of my love and not a reflection of me!

The realization of that moment with God changed everything and was why she and Paul were now at an impasse.

"Hello...earth to Aleeya! Honey, are you still there?" Paul's deep voice disrupted her thoughts.

"Oh...I'm sorry...what were you saying?" Aleeya said, surprised by his quick return to the phone.

"When will you be home?" Paul stated in an edgy tone that Aleeya immediately picked up on.

"Paul, you sound upset. What's wrong? Who were you talking to?"

"No one...everything's fine. So, what time?"

"Well, I wish I could tell you in ten minutes, but I can't. I'm on my way to a family in crisis."

Aleeya halfway wished they had discussed this before the interruption. His whole mood had changed, leaving her wondering exactly who was the *no one* on the other line.

"*AGAIN!*" Paul shouted into the receiver.

"Well, sweetheart, I told you I'm on call all this week, and since there's a crisis with one of my families, I-I have to go." Aleeya flinched as a sudden queasiness made her stomach clinched.

"Aleeya Rochelle Thomas… Tell me that you ain't putting the needs of one of them nasty…"

Aleeya cringed at the way Paul so descriptively depicted her clients. Thank God, they couldn't hear him.

"Trailer trash clients in front of your own man's needs." Paul bit out in anger.

Anytime he used her full name and other choice words, she was in for a fight. Speaking in an even pitch, Aleeya tried to mask the hurt rising in her voice. "Paul, it's not even like that, and you know it. I'm on call. This is my job. I'm sorry, but I have to go."

"No, Artie…don't give me that crap. This situation is totally unacceptable, do you hear me? Unacceptable! I will not allow my woman to play me as second fiddle to some nut case."

Rolling her eyes heavenward, Aleeya drew a few deep, calming breaths she often encouraged her clients to take. Paul was definitely taking things too far with his condescending tone, chiding her as if she were a child. It was insulting. "Hold up, Paul! I realize you're upset but let's get a couple of things straight. Number one, I'm not putting anything before you. Number two, this is my job, and even though I don't want to go to a roach-infested trailer to deal with someone else's drama tonight, I have to." Her voice trembled with indignation.

"What I think you need to get straight is, number one, your priorities. Because I will not, and let me be clear, I will not remain in a relationship with anyone who can so easily toss my feelings and needs aside."

"*EXCUSE YOU!*" Aleeya gasped, thinking Paul must have completely lost his mind. Since the beginning of their relationship, she had made him her priority. For the last year, she had practically been taking care of his lazy butt because, for some odd reason, he couldn't seem to keep a full-time job to save his neck. In the last year of their relationship, she stupidly allowed him to convince her that they should live together in her two-bedroom apartment.
He claimed he would occupy the second bedroom, yeah, that lasted all of two days. Still, as he explained, it was all okay because, after all, they'd be married before the year was out.

Well, that year came and went, and so did all those promising job opportunities he was pursuing. In essence, she was taking care of her man and then some. She was paying all their household expenses, car notes, not to mention putting herself through school and financing his numerous *ministry* trips to Arizona. She was burning the candle at both ends just to keep them afloat, and he had the nerve to question her priorities.

"Paul, you want to talk about needs, well what about what *I* need? Have you ever considered for one moment the just maybe you're neglecting my needs?"

"Oh, here we go with this. I need you to marry me crap. I've told you a thousand times it's just a piece of paper. If you want to be technical about it, in biblical times, two people were considered married after having sex, so I guess we've been married for at least a year and a half." He sarcastically snickered.

Aleeya could feel her eyes fill with tears as the brashness of his words shot through her heart like an arrow through an apple, leaving a gaping hole in its wake. Who was this man that she still professed to be madly in love with?

For goodness' sake, they both knew that sex didn't make a marriage. Besides, it wasn't the sex that she prized the most. It was committing oneself to another person before God and remaining faithful to that one person no matter what. That was the substance that good marriages were founded on, and that's what she wanted…with Paul. She only wished she'd had come to that conclusion before she let Paul into her life and, eventually, her bed. Did she want to be Paul's wife? Absolutely, but she also wanted Paul to desire to be a husband …her husband.

Then tell him that, tell him what you really need from him!

Aleeya paused. Could she really be that bold? Could she really put her feeling out there like that for Paul to, see? What if he didn't say what she was hoping to hear? What if he flat-out rejected her? What would she do then?

You need to know where he stands so you can decide whether to keep riding this train or get off at the next stop.

As Aleeya heard Jordi's words swirling in her head, she swallowed past the lump rising in her throat. She had to do this! She had to lay all her cards on the table once and for all. So, with a boldness she didn't realize she possessed she cleared her throat and spoke up.

"Look Paul, we are not married, not in God's eyes, not in the eyes of the church, and definitely not in my eyes. I need you to stop playing games and show me you really care by putting a ring on my finger, and making me officially your wife like you promised to do over a year ago. As a matter-of-fact, if you had kept *that* promise, we wouldn't be having *this* discussion now." She stated boldly, although her body was trembling with every word. She hadn't intended on saying all that to him, but now that it was out, she couldn't and wouldn't turn back.

"You know what, Artie...ever since you left Temple of Praise a year ago and started attending this new church and hanging out with Jordin, you've been talking crazy. Before, everything between us was great. Now, I'm nothing but a player to you and a guy who apparently doesn't keep his word." Paul's tone held so much contempt that Aleeya could hardly believe he was the same man who moments ago said he missed her.

"Paul, that's not what I'm trying to say...." Aleeya tried to interject, but Paul talked right over her.

"All you women ever do is cry and whine about being married and your biological clocks ticking. But when you get a good man, you don't even know how to talk to them, let alone treat them. Well, I got some news for you, sweetheart, you might want to be my wife, but as far as I'm concerned, you're not wife material. Matter-of-fact, I'm tired of this entire situation...you know what, we're done!"

"I'm not wife material? He did not just say that to me!" Aleeya seeing red, was about to come back with the mother of all comebacks when she heard a pronounced click in her ear.

"Hello...*HELLO!*" Her mind exploded. "Did this broke, behind punk just hang up on me? And no less with the phone I bought him? Oh no he didn't!!!" Aleeya shouted a string of obscenities she knew she'd have to repent for later. "And what did he mean we're done? Done with what...us? This man ain't got a job the first, had to borrow money off me so he could eat when he took his last trip down to Phoenix, and he has the nerve to try and quit me...Boy please! Aleeya thought gripping the steering wheel as she tied to drive and regulate her breathing simultaneously. The absolute nerve of him being done with her when she had given him everything, and now when she wanted to cash in on her years of investing into his life, he decides to dump her? Oh, that ain't happening, she fumed.

We're done!

The finality of his word weighed on her heart like a ton of bricks. Suddenly a surge of panic replaced the rage within. After two long years, they were through...done... finished for *good*! Hot tears gushed down her cheeks as her breath caught on a painful sob that swelled in the back of her throat. He was throwing her away, throwing out their relationship like it was yesterday's trash. How could he do this to her, to the future they often talked about having together?

How could he say she wasn't wife material when he had just told her last week that he had never loved another woman like he loved her? Okay, granted, they were in bed at the time, but he still seemed sincere. How could calling him on the carpet about marriage cause this break? Aleeya's vision blurred as she rounded the curve of a dimly lit street. Doing the only thing she knew to do she cried out to God in anguish.

"Father...why? I've already lost mom, please don't take Paul away from me too. I'm so close to having my dream. Please don't let it turn into a nightmare." She prayed through her tears as her stomach clinched again. How would she explain to her family that Paul had dumped her after just announcing to her cousin Keera Jefferies last week that a wedding announcement was on the horizon? She could only imagine what Keera would say.

"Girl, you just let the best thing that will likely ever happen to you walk straight out the door after two years of hard labor...time, and money. I told you this was going to happen if you kept acting like Miss Goodie Two Shoes. You of all people know black women over thirty ain't got too many men looking at them anyway. Shoot, now that you're a Christian, you done turned uppity. But mark my words, Artie, you keep messing around, and you're gonna be like all those other holier-than-thou women in the church...who are old and alone!"

Panic filled her heart as her cousin words washed over her. She had just turned thirty-one last month and God knew she didn't want to be one of those holy-roller spinsters she had made fun of when she was a kid.

Maybe she had acted too hastily, and her words were too harsh, Aleeya surmised. After all, she and Paul were practically married, and given time, he probably would've gotten her to the altar—*eventually*. She knew he was trying to get himself established in the music industry, and as he said, some things just took time. Aleeya's hit the redial button on her phone and waited impatiently as it rang and rang. When it finally picked up, it was his voice mail, causing a new wave of anger to overwhelm her.

OH! How dare he not answer my call? Aleeya thought hotly, furious that he was using her own ignoring tactic against her. Spotting an entranceway wide enough for her to turn around, she aimed her car in that direction. She was about to make a quick U-turn when she noticed the sign to her left, it was Edgewood Trailer Park...Sherri Kincaid's trailer park. She jerked her wheel to the right with a heavy sigh and headed toward Sherri's trailer...*duty calls!*

Return to Jericho

Chapter One

"I will not leave you comfortless." John 14:18

Five years later...

"Great, I'm going to be late now." Aleeya heaved a sigh while tapping a rhythmic beat with her fingers on the steering wheel. It was a sticky first day in Hawaii. It was only ten in the morning but already a sunny, eighty-two degrees. Swiping at her brow, she continued to mumble. "Maybe I shouldn't have waited for that extra whip cream on my salted caramel latte", she mused while her eyes perused the parking lot for the tenth time, looking for any open spaces. Looking in the rear-view mirror, she looked at her puffy eyes still tinged with pink. Averting her gaze, she sighed heavily. It wasn't the fluffy mound of cream that caused her to be running late. She hadn't anticipated having a crying spell that morning. Feeling the sensation of tears beginning to burn at the back of her eyelids again, she inhaled deeply, then let the air burst out of her with a hard sigh. "It is what it is." She said, while relaxing the death grip she had on the steering wheel. "Things don't always work out like you think," she said diplomatically, staring at the palm trees swaying in the breeze. Noting that, for some reason, the ones here looked greener and more robust than the ones back home in Florida.

Waking up in Hawaii, Aleeya felt both joy and sorrow. As she stepped out on her hotel balcony, before sunrise, the smell of the salty ocean mist greeted her nose. Her eyes couldn't help but be amazed as she watched the seagulls fly high in the air singing their song of praise right before nose diving into the depth of the ocean to retrieve their morning meal. But what was truly breathtaking was how the sky displayed such a kaleidoscope of colours right before the sun appeared to take its rightful place in the sky. "Only in paradise." Aleeya mused as the warm sun beat down on her bare shoulders. "It can't get much better than this?" But before the words were out of her mouth, a dark thought spoke up.

"Yeah, it could, especially if you were here with Paul like you originally planned!" The dark thought prodded.

Immediately her heart came crashing down, hitting her stomach with a great big thud. This would have been her and ex-fiancé's, Paul's fifth wedding anniversary, and their son or daughter would have just turned five. Automatically touching the area where the scar on her abdomen lay, Aleeya swallowed beyond the lump of emotions forming in her throat. If only her and Paul had not quarrelled that night. If only she had listened to her conscience and not gone to the Kincaid's home. If only Terry Kincaid wouldn't have been there drunk and in a rage. If only…if only. She bit back the curse word that was itching to leap off her tongue. She pursed her lips tight, not even allowing air to flow through them for the moment. She and God had done a lot of work in the last two years battling her swearing habit, and there was no way she was going another ten rounds with that demon again.

"I will keep you in perfect peace if your mind stays on me."

"Yes...Lord," Aleeya quickly agreed with the scripture that rose in her mind. "Come on, Lelee...think on something else," she spoke to herself in the quietness of the car, trying to distract her mind from any more unpleasant thoughts. "Think on something lovely... I'm in paradise. What is praiseworthy? I am about to speak at the juvenile offender's conference about my therapeutic program for delinquent youth. This is a new day for me. God, you are so good. No more talking about the past. I'm thinking about what is true...Paul left me. I've already forgiven him. There is no need to continue to dwell on it. It is part of the past." She concluded.

"Oh...really? Then why were you crying this morning?" A familiar voice said.

Aleeya kept looking straight ahead as if she didn't hear the familiar feminine voice coming from the passenger seat of her car.

"Girl, don't be trying to ignore me. You know I'm not going anywhere until you answer my question."

Aleeya blew out a sigh and slowly looked to her right. There sat her mother, Betty Thomas, in the passenger seat looking lovely in her lavender-colored dress with a smile as big as Texas gracing her face. "Lord, why is this happening to me?" Aleeya cried out, slapping her hand to her forehead. Her mother had been long dead for the last seven years. However, somehow Betty didn't get the message and still decided to hang around, popping up at the most inconvenient moments. It didn't happen all the time, only when she was stressed, which seemed like a lot lately or when making a big decision. Like clockwork, her mom would inevitably show up. The first time she visibly saw her mother, she thought she was losing her marbles. Swallowing her pride, one day, she confided in her friend Ted Sikes. As a Christian therapist and colleague at her university, she was sure he had heard it all. So, she spilled the beans, of which Ted quickly reassured her that she wasn't going crazy.

"Aleeya, what your experiencing is perfectly normal. It's called bereavement hallucinations. Elderly widows experience this phenomenon all the time," Ted reassured.

So, there was a name for it. She only wished it came with a shutoff valve.

"Well, Lelee girl, I'm waiting?"

"This is not really happening. You are not real. You are a figment of my imagination," Aleeya said aloud, then looked to her right again to see her mother's smiling face still sitting there.

"Peak-a-boo, I see you baby girl." She said, raising her hands and shaking them for added effect.

"Mom, why are you here? Why aren't you in heaven walking streets of gold and enjoying your mansion...asking Eve why she ate that piece of fruit?"

"Girl, I got all eternity to do all that. But you need my help, so I asked God, and he said I could come for a spell, so here I am," she said, while looking around. "So, this is the world's version of paradise? Hum, it's no heaven, honey I can tell you that right now."

Aleeya looked back out the windshield then just shook her head. "You know they have angels for that sort of thing, not to mention the Holy Spirit; he is, after all, the counselor and comforter."

"Yeah, you know I met the Holy Spirit... he's really great. I wish I would have taken better advantage of his counsel while on earth. Lelee, you really should make a point of hooking up with him more often."

"Wow...this is perfect, absolutely perfect." Aleeya shut her eyes and shook her head.

"Girl, will you answer the question. I don't want to spend all day down here with you. I got to meet up with your Aunt Katherine and your Uncle Billy later."

"Ma, what question?"

"Lelee, don't be playing with me." She gave Aleeya her famous no-nonsense glance. "You know perfectly well what I asked and why I asked it."

"Okay, fine...I guess I was crying over what could have been but never was. Why Paul up and left, why Terry Kincaid...." She pressed her lips tightly before speaking again. "Why did any of that fiasco have to happen!!!"

Aleeya had believed she was past this hurtful place in her life until that moment, but apparently, she wasn't.

Five years ago, choices were made that she had no control over, but those choices and the people who made them wrecked the plans she had made for her life. That one fateful night had turned her life on its ear. It was the reason she had to wake up in paradise alone instead of a wife and mother.

"Paul was the one who said let's save up and go to Hawaii for our fifth wedding anniversary. Then when we have one lousy disagreement, he walks away from the life we could've had together. Like it was nothing." Aleeya growled.

"Baby, what makes you think you would have made it to your fifth year of marriage. Lelee, I've always told you, when people show you who they are, honey, believe them."

"I know...I know, but we could've had something good...something special."

"Shoulda...coulda...woulda...but didn't. Instead of crying over what you lost, honey, you need to be thanking God for what he kept you from. And if you don't, honey, I sure will. God, I thank you for keeping my baby girl safe from the snare of the enemy. Jesus, thank you for making a way out of no way. Thank you, Spirit of God, for rescuing her from physical and spiritual death. Hallelujah. Thank you for sending your warring angels to keep her protected. Father, I thank you."

When Aleeya started thanking and praising God with her mother, she didn't know; however, by the time she was done and opened her eyes, she was alone in the car. The fragrance of God's sweet presence still lingered in the small space. Grabbing a tissue from her purse, she dabbed at the last tear from her eye just in time to see an available parking space in the next row. Gunning the engine and putting her total weight on the gas pedal, Aleeya made a sharp turn. With screeching tires, she quickly overtook the spot from the navy-blue SUV coming down the same row.

"Ha-ha, sucker beat ya to it," she openly mocked, then covered her mouth. "Oops, sorry Lord, that wasn't at all Christlike." Shrugging a shoulder, she vowed to do better. Turning off the car, she unbuckled her seat belt and swung open the door in one flowing motion. "Girl, I swear you would be late to your own funeral." She fussed at herself as she bent over to retrieve her purse and Starbucks carrier from the passenger seat. Backing out of the car, she deposited her coffee cup on the hood to retrieve the workshop materials she was presenting for the conference from the back seat. For a moment, she paused in thought.

"Wow, Lord, … I'm presenting the program you gave me at an international conference and in all places…Hawaii. God, you're so awesome." She smiled, looking toward the sky. "Who would have ever thought the girl from the hood in Jericho City would finally land on her feet?" Shaking her head in amazement. "Can't get much better than this."

Well, it could if you had a man sharing that enormous suite with you.

Aleeya rolled her eyes at the nagging thought. Satan wasn't going to take a backseat to her moment of victory as he reminded her of her cousin's words.

Kylie's Harris remarks rang in her head like a blaring fire alarm. So what? She was single in paradise. She was sure she wasn't the first and would definitely not be the last. Yes, she was single with no man in sight. She was thirty-five, never married, and had no kids. She was tired of defending her single status to her cousins. "There are plenty of married women I know who never had the chance to even go to Hawaii. If God is allowing me to go as a single, well, so be it." She remembered saying to the lip-smacking, eye-rolling, and head-shaking perturbed cousins. Well, she didn't care if they liked it or not. This was her life, and this was how she planned on living it.

Feeling her confidence swell, she put the last bag on her shoulder and a box under her arm. She snagged the coffee cup off her hood, whacked the car door with her hip, and spun around only to collide with a hard-green wall complete with legs and arms. "Oh my God!" Startled, she bounced off him and hit the car with such force that her coffee went flying toward him, splashing them both with the semi-lukewarm liquid. Embarrassed beyond belief, Aleeya wished she could seep through the cracks of the concrete just like her latte was doing. Frantic to correct her clumsiness, she searched for some napkins or something to clean up her mess.

"Oh, my goodness, sir...I'm so very sorry," she said in a panic as she rummaged through her bags, trying to locate something to wipe up the coffee. The only thing she had was the scarf she wrapped her braids in to keep them in place. "Sir, I am extremely sorry for making a mess on you." She apologized profusely, too mortified to look him in the face. She just bent over, wiping down his bare legs. *Dude has nice legs*, she mused to herself. As if God was chastising her for her semi-naughty thought, she fell into him again as the weight of the bags shifted forward.

"Miss, that's really not necessary." His amused tenor rang overhead.

"No…no, this was clearly my fault," she said, flustered by what she had done. "I should've been watching where I was turning. I'll be happy to pay for any dry cleaning. She offered, still bent over trying to rectify her faux pas.

"I don't think they will dry clean my legs." He chuckled good-naturedly. "And to be honest, the fault was mine. When I saw you with all those heavy bags, I rushed over to help but startled you in the process," he said, reaching down and taking the heavy bags off her shoulders, then extended his hand toward her so she could stand up.

Taking the hand offered, Aleeya stood up, ready to apologize again but stop mid-sentence as she gazed at her rescuer. She quickly inhaled as recognition filled her thoughts. After twenty-five years, how in the world had she managed to bump into her junior high crush, Jenus T Ballard, from her hometown Jericho?

Chapter Two

Jenus, or JT as he was called back then, was her first serious crush when she was an eighth-grader in junior high. Back then, she was nothing more than a flat-chested, skinny, freckle-faced geek. At the same time, Jenus was Jericho's star quarterback, team captain, a senior, and the cutest guy she'd ever laid eyes on. All the girls swooned over him whenever he walked by, and she was no different. She would always stare at him in the halls whenever he passed with his crew. Not that he'd ever notice her....no one ever did. But one day she was returning her book to the library she rounded the corner and he collided with her in the hallway, much like she had done to him today. He knocked her down spilling his Gatorade all over her. His entourage, who always hung with him, laughed it up and ribbed him for being a klutz. He good-naturedly took the ribbing as he bent down to help her up.

"Sorry about that, kiddo. Did I hurt you?"

Too enamored to speak, she looked up at him through her dripping bangs and shook her head no.

"Here, why don't you take my towel and dry yourself off." He offered. Reaching for it, she then hesitated. "But won't you need it for the game?" It was a stupid thing to say. The school had hundreds of those hand towels lying around, and she was sure the football team captain could get as many as he wanted.

"Don't sweat it…. kid."

She wanted to keep the conversation going, knowing that none of her friends would ever believe that she had actually spoken to JT Ballard. Wanting him to know she thought he was a great football player, she blurted out the first thing that came to mind. Unfortunately, what was in her head and what came out of her mouth made her cringe. "I think you're a great catch."

"Yeah, so does my girlfriend Shelia, freckles." That made his entire crew break out in laughter and generated more teasing about him dumping the prom queen to be with a freckle face kid.

"Shut up! Let's get out of here before we're late," he said and walked away, not even giving her a backward glance.

Just as quick as it happened her encounter with her secret crush was over. Hurrying to the bathroom she used a fist full of paper towels to dry off. She wouldn't dare use the towel the star quarterback gave her to do such a task. Gently folded it, Aleeya put it in her pocket with a plan on keeping it until the day she died or at least got a real boyfriend.

Now even after all these years, the man still possessed a magnetic charisma. The fact that he was still absolutely gorgeous didn't hurt either. His deep caramel complexion glistened in the sun. His unshaven appearance gave him a rugged manly look about him, accentuated by his chiselled square chin with a cleft right smack in the middle. His deep dimples popped as he smiled down at her. Then there were those eyes. The most dazzling forest green eyes bore into hers. Aleeya tried standing taller, feeling her knees beginning to wobble. Realizing she hadn't said anything for a while, she commanded herself to quit gawking at the man and speak.

"Umm...I umm...appreciate your willingness to help me," she managed to say. "I guess chivalry is not dead. You're certainly proof of that. I hope your run-in with me hasn't spoiled your willingness to help another damsel in distress." She nervously babbled inwardly, wishing she'd stop.

"No harm, no foul." He shrugged it off. "Oh...by the way, my name is JT...and you are?"

"He doesn't remember me? Well, of course, he doesn't, you goofball, it had been at least twenty-five years ago, and to your credit...a lot has changed." She though and thanked the good Lord for that, growth spurt in all the right places, not to mention braces. "Well, I guess it's only right for you to know the name of the person who splashed coffee all over you...it's Ale...Artie Thomas." She always gave out her nickname just in case he was a stalker.

"Artie, it's a pleasure." He smiled, gently squeezing the hand he already held while adjusting her bags on his shoulders. "I take it from all this." He eyed her bags. "This is more of a business than a pleasure trip?"

"It's a bit of both," she confessed. "There's an international conference being held this week, and I'm one of the speakers. I'll be doing a workshop this afternoon and tomorrow morning. I came early today to get set up so I could catch some of the morning sessions. But at this rate, I don't think that's going to happen."

"Is this your first conference?" He asked, stepping out of her way so she could pass him.

"Yes, it is." She smiled with the confession as they fell in step, walking toward the conference center. "Are you part of the conference?" She inquired, doubting it based on his leisure attire.

"Yeah. This is my fourth conference and third time presenting," he said, pointing to the suit of clothing he held in his arms along with her bags.

"Wait…are these the clothes you're wearing to the conference? Let's switch," she suggested feeling inwardly guilty for being so critical of her rescuer. "I will hold your suit so it won't get wrinkled by my bags," she insisted, already taking garment bag from his hand.

"Okay, thanks! By the way, don't worry about being late. I can guarantee you that normally most of these things never start on time."

"Well, that makes me feel a lot better since I'm talking to a pro," she complimented, hoping she wasn't coming off as too forward. "When do you present?"

"Oh, about ten minutes ago." He chuckled at her surprised expression. "Yeah, I'm running a bit late myself."

"Oh, my goodness…you're late because of me. JT, I'm so sorry," she said, feeling awful.

"Don't give it another thought. I'm late because I decided to do some paddleboarding this morning. So, my tardiness is no one's fault but my own." He casually smiled down at her. "Besides, I'm not by myself this year. I have a whole team with me so they can fill in while I help you set up."

"No, absolutely not. I have wasted too much of your time as it is."

"You're anything but a waste of my time Artie." His voice dropped low as his dimples deepened with his smile.

Blushing, Aleeya cleared her throat. It had been a long time since a man had paid her any attention, so for that man to be JT Ballard, her sweet junior high crush, wow! *To all my classmates…eat your heart out*, she thought.

"So, what workshop will you be speaking at?" She inquired, noticing how he automatically took the position of walking on the outside curb. "A gentleman too...*Lawd,* have mercy." She inwardly squealed.

"My workshop is the rehabilitation of offending juveniles."

"That's the one I was hoping to attend." she said, enthused.

"Well, you're in luck. I know for certain that the best part of the presentation can't be done without me." He chuckled. "Why don't we get your work area set up, then we'll go in together...deal?"

"Deal." She smiled as she took the arm he offered and crossed the walkway together thinking to herself, *"This morning started off bitter, but it is getting sweeter by and by"*.

Chapter Three

"A time to mourn and a time to dance". Eccl 3:4

For the life of him, Jenus had no idea what had come over him when bumping into Artie that morning. He wasn't the flirtations type. Usually, to keep from giving women the wrong impression, as a rule, he didn't go out of his way like today to help a damsel in distress. Not that he wasn't a gentleman, it's just that women these days seemed to take the simplest of gestures from a guy and blow it up into a marriage proposal. But from the moment he laid eyes on Artie Thomas, he sensed something was peculiar about her and oddly familiar. Something about her eyes immediately placed him at ease. He noticed she wasn't overly made up like most of the women at the conference. She just had a fresh, natural look with just a hint of freckles across the bridge of her nose. He didn't know why that little detail stuck with him, but it made him like her all the more. The coffee spill was a minor mishap that yielded a significant reward, especially when she looked at him with those bright, cinnamon-colored eyes. He couldn't recall seeing anyone with eyes that brilliant before. Something about her tugged at his heart. Why else would he ask her out on a date?

Wow, he couldn't believe it. The last date he had been on was seven years ago with his fiancée Nyla Greer. Taking a moment, he blew out a long steadying breath. "I miss you babe; Lord knows I do." He coughed clearing his throat of emotion. Nyla was only a year or two older than Aleeya and just as beautiful. Losing her to gun violence hurt. Knowing his son Trevor's gang banging ways had a role in her death grieved him beyond words. Nyla was dead trying to save his son Trevor who still lived. In some ways his grief was unending. But right now, was not the time to think of what he had lost. He had mourned for years but tonight, he wanted to dance. Looking at himself one more time in the mirror, he smiled at his reflection.

"You're going for the knockout punch with this one." He laughed at himself. He was definitely dressing to impress with his dark gray knitted shirt and black dress pants that showed off his trim physique. "Not bad for forty-two," he said placing his watch on his wrist as he thought back to that morning. They were extremely late for his presentation. They had gotten lost in the endless row of doors that led to every room but hers. By the time they located Artie's room and got set up, his presentation was over. Not that he cared, he knew his team would do well without him. It just gave him more time with Artie. After setting up, he stayed for her presentation and then took her to lunch. Halfway through lunch, he was already fishing for some way to entice her to go to dinner with him but was taken by surprise when she asked him first.

"Welcome to the modern world where women take the lead." He smirked. Admittedly it was a little refreshing but he was still a little old fashion and like to be the pursuer.

The little jazz club he was planning on taking her to had been one of his favorite spots since discovering it last year. She seemed excited and eager to go when he told her about it. He only prayed she'd enjoy the experience as much as he did. They would meet up at six in the hotel lobby. Looking at his watch he, winced. It was five forty-five. Even though they were in the same hotel, he was on the thirtieth floor. It was evening time, so everyone would be heading out, meaning a longer wait time to catch an elevator going down. Snagging his wallet, hotel key card, and phone, he was out the door and made it to the elevator in a few short strides.

Hitting the down button, he was pleasantly surprised that he needed to wait only a few moments before the door opened. With his head down, he stepped into the crowded elevator. With his back toward everyone, and phone in hand, he checked his messages. The first five were from his Trevor's mom and at least six from Eagle Crest Academy. His stomach tensed as it usually did anytime, he received texts from either. If Cheryl was calling, that meant something was going on with their son. If it was coming from Eagle Crest, that indicated a problem was about to explode at the academy.

Tonight, he didn't want to be bothered by either. He just wanted to be a guy who met a beautiful woman in paradise and hopefully would have a good time out on the town.

As more people entered and exited the elevator, he found himself shuffled toward the rear until his back connected with something very soft. A soft clearing of the throat alerted him to the fact that he was invading someone's space. Before he could turn to apologize, he heard her soft feminine alto speak up.

"Well, I guess my second impression on you, Mr. Ballard, has lacked luster." A woman's voice spoke up from behind him.

Craning his neck to the side to see who said that, he was startled to see Artie. Twisting around to face her, he immediately noticed how amazing she looked in her black spaghetti-strapped dressed and leopard-print heels. Her long braids were in an updo, and the flora scent she wore was making his insides jump. Her lovely face was graced with a little more makeup than what she had worn that morning, but it was not overdone. What stood out more than her beautiful sparkling eyes was her lushes' lips that showcased her breathtaking smile. "Hey, you." He smiled down over her.

"Hey yourself."

He was never one to like tight spaces, but he was definitely not complaining now. The crowded elevator made the looks they exchanged with each other entrancing as if they were the only people there. An impulse to kiss her was the only thought rummaging through his mind, so to keep from acting on the urge, he spoke up.

"Let me assure you, Ms. Thomas, as far as second impressions go, you lack nothing." He swept an unruly braid out of her face. "The only reason I didn't spot you immediately is due to this annoying little trinket that is going off in my pocket as we speak." He placed the phone on silent and quickly stashed it in his pants pocket. "It will only reappear in case of an emergency of which there couldn't possibly be anything happening important enough for me to take my eyes off you." He pledged.

"Oh, my word, you are a charmer." She gave her best rendition of a southern woman's accent, then smiled, taking the arm he extended her. "I think I'm going to call on some of those old grandmother prayers and hymns I learned as a little girl to keep my wits around you tonight." They both laughed.

"Not to worry, my dear…you are perfectly safe with me. I'm a good ole Christian boy. So, dinner and jazz music are all I'm offering…tonight."

"Well, that's refreshing to hear, seeing I'm also a good ole Christian girl, so a good dinner, scintillating conversation, and at least one dance is all I want…tonight." She flirted back as the elevator emptied, and he led her into the hotel lobby.

"Wait, who said anything about dancing?" He playfully furrowed his brows as they strolled to the concierge desk, Jenus enjoying the light touch of her arm, holding on to his.

"Well, the way I see it, one dance will be your penitence for not noticing me in the elevator." She playfully pouted. "Especially after I spent hours getting ready just to impress you."

"I see," he said, stopping their playful banter as he approached the hotel concierge.

"Yes, Mr. Ballard, how can I assist you?" The concierge inquired.

"Please have my car brought up."

"Right away, sir, and I hope you and your date have a pleasant evening."

"Thanks, we will." He smiled, turning away and walking them both toward the hotel's main entrance to wait for his car. *Date*, again the word brought Nyla's face to mind, but the heartache was a little less this time as he felt Aleeya's delicate fingers in the palm of his hand.

For everything, there is a season, a time for every purpose under heaven: a time to be born and a time to die, a time to mourn, and a time to dance.

The Bible verse from Ecclesiastes chapter three rose up in his heart like a sweet song. He and Nyla loved to dance. Well, tonight, he'd have a new dance partner to make new memories with.

"I see you're getting quiet on me, Mr. Ballard. You're not trying to wiggle your way out of the dance you owe me tonight, are you?"

"On the contrary, Artie. Although you do drive a hard bargain, I'm willing to accept your terms…I might even throw a second dance if you play your cards right." He teased, taking her hand in the crook of his arm and holding it tight, noticing an intense jolt of electricity shooting up his arm.

"Why, Mr. Ballard, what would a good ole Christian boy like yourself know about playing cards? I would think you would shun gambling of any kind," she playfully scolded.

"First off, I never play with real money, so technically, it's not gambling," he admonished. The strange pulsating tingle from his fingertips resonated all the way up to his arm. He prayed it was a sign of attraction and not something else. *"God, please don't let this be a sign of a heart attack."* He whispered the prayer.

Something was oddly familiar about this woman. He had racked his brain all evening trying to place her; finally, he gave up and took a nap. "Maybe it's just the fact I've been so out of touch that I've forgotten what it felt like to be attracted to someone." He mused within his heart.

"Okay, then if you don't play for money, what do you play for?" Aleeya inquired.

Her question broke into his wayward thoughts. "A bag of pretzel M&M's and on rare occasions, extra dances."

"Oh…so how exactly do I play this card game of yours, Mr. Ballard?" She smiled up at him.

"Well, for starters, Artie, how about calling me Jenus…Mr. Ballard is my dad's name. JT is a nickname I've long out grown."

"Jenus, wow. So, we're on a first name basis now, are we? Well, if I know your first name, you should know mine. It's Aleeya."

He furrowed his brows again, looking down at her. "Aleeya is a beautiful name. I don't understand how you get Artie out of that?"

"Okay, the short version of this story is, my middle name is Rochelle, and as you know, my last name is Thomas so, string it all together, and you get Art. However, when I was younger, I had several male cousins who loved giving out stupid nicknames, so mine became…."

"Let me guess, Artie McFartie." He let out a belly laugh and was rewarded with a playful punch in the arm.

"I swear, guys must have some secret club to torture us defenseless young females with." She put her free hand on her hip.

"Yeah, we do. It's called the he-man woman-haters club. Didn't you ever watch The Little Rascals?" He chuckled as his car came around and stopped in front of them. The valet promptly jumped out as Jenus open the door on the passenger side and helped Aleeya in.

"I hope you know by calling me by that ridiculous name, you've just upped the ante to two additional dances," she said just before he shut the door and trotted around the front of the car to get in the driver's seat.

Buckling himself in, he glanced at her quickly before pulling out into traffic. "I'm sure by the time the night is over, we will have danced half of the night away...Aleeya." He smiled, strategizing to dance to every slow song the band would play, looking forward to the closeness of her in his arms.

Chapter Four

"Forgetting the past and looking forward to what lies ahead." Philippians 3:13 NLT

The mixture of sweet spice and fried food filled the air. The dim lighting, and small round tables with lit candles as their centerpiece, gave the jazz club an intimate and cozy vibe.

This is so perfect! Aleeya thought to herself as she rested her chin on her entwined fingers, smiling just for the sheer fact that she was straying far from her norm. She loved live jazz but hadn't gone to a place like this since ending things with Paul. Instinctively she touched her abdomen. It had been five years, and she had done a great deal of healing, physically and emotionally. However, sometimes, especially when she was having a lonely moment, memories of what could have been still haunted her.

"Don't go there," Aleeya commanded herself, allowing the memory of her past hurts to fade as the music ended. She refused to ruin a perfect evening with Jenus by thinking about what could've been. Just saying Jenus's name brought her back to her happy place.

"I can't believe how great he looks after all this time," she muttered to herself while scanning the room, giving everybody and everything the once over. Turning back to her table, she jumped, seeing her mom's smiling face.

"Humph! This is nice. This boy got some taste. You better keep him close."

"Mom…oh my God…what are you doing here?" Aleeya looked around to see if her date was about to return to their table.

"Get a grip. Nobody can see or hear me but you. You know I ain't nothing but a…hum what did that therapist tell you, a hallucination. Humph, these so-called professionals sure do come up with some crazy stuff to explain the supernatural."

"Mom!" Aleeya rolled her eyes. She loved her mother dearly, but popping in on her and of all times, the first actual date she had in five years was unreal.

"I'm just checking in. Seeing how your day is going," her mother said, looking around the room.

Aleeya eyed her mother with suspicion. "Ma…what are you really doing here?" she questioned.

"What, I'm a citizen of Heaven now, so you can't associate with me anymore?" Her mother pursed her lips and rolled her eyes. "And we used to be so close."

"Mom…really." Aleeya chuckled. She was right about that they were so close. Mother and daughter, they were, but the relationship forged between them was so much more. Betty was her greatest cheerleader, confidant, counselor, critic, teacher, mentor…she could go on and on. They had planned to travel the world together just as soon as she completed her master's in counseling. Well, that dream never came.

It was just supposed to be a routine doctor's visit. The next thing they knew, Betty had to go to a lung specialist, and within four months, her mom died of lung cancer. Then an angel of light walked into her life named Paul Tate. Too bad she couldn't see him for the foul demon that he was.

"Now, Lelee…don't start thinking about that knuckle-head. It'll ruin the entire evening me and Jesus got planned for you."

"First off, Ma…I'm sure Jesus would disapprove of you calling people knuckle-heads. And second, what do you mean you and Jesus planned this evening?"

"Well, to answer your first question, who do you think gave Paul that name in the first place?" Betty pursed her lips and rolled her eyes, causing Aleeya to giggle. "And to answer your second question. God let me see a whole bunch of stuff while I'm up there in heaven, including this day, and I could hardly wait to see your response to it. Oh, by the way, you can thank me for spilling that coffee on him too." Her mom winked.

"Mama!" Aleeya bucked her eyes.

"What?" Her mom gave her a *'what of it?'* look. "Girl, please, that boy knocked you on your behind and splashed his drink on you in the eighth grade. I told Jesus that would be a cute way for you to meet up again. Plus, get a little payback." Betty covered her mouth, snickering.

Aleeya couldn't help but bow her head and chuckle too. "Ma...I swear they are going to kick you right out of heaven."

"Oh no, they won't." She rolled her neck. "I'm in there now, and I ain't fittin to be put out. Besides, all these crazy folks left here on earth. Shoot, honey, the good Lord ain't got time to be worrying about little ole me." She winked. "Oops...here comes your young man. Now straighten your shoulders and stop slouching. Let the man see you're not that same flat-chested girl he knocked over in Jericho."

"Oh, my Lord." Aleeya bowed her head in embarrassment. How was it that her mom was long gone but still able to cause her cheeks to flush pink? Seeing Jenus on his way back to their table, she let out a slow breath, allowing the hammering in her chest to ease. Turning back around, Aleeya found that her mother was gone. All she could hear was the soft whisper of her voice saying, *have fun.*

Fun was always a luxury Aleeya believed she couldn't afford, but maybe just this one time, she could.

Taking a deep breath, she exhaled, giving herself permission to relax as she savored every moment. The saxophone's melody was relaxing and soothed her tired soul. Closing her eyes, Aleeya began swaying to the tune, as the memory of how great slow dancing in the warmth of Jenus' embrace felt. If anyone ever told her that twenty-five years later, she'd be in the arms of her schoolgirl crush, she would've laughed them to scorn. But here she was, loving every minute of it.

"Don't tell me you're already tired!" Jenus said, coming up from behind.

"No, I'm not tired, just enjoying myself," Aleeya said, accepting the light cola he offered her. After taking a few sips, she added. "By the way, you're not too shabby on the dance floor. I'm impressed."

"Why, thank you, madam," he said, executing a mock bow before taking his chair, causing Aleeya to giggle. "You weren't so bad out there yourself."

"Yeah, right!" Aleeya rolled her eyes and waved off his compliment. "You just made me look good."

"You definitely don't need my help in that department. You look good all by yourself," he said in a soft but bold tone without looking away; his gaze reflected his evident appreciation of her looks.

"Thank you," Aleeya said softly, dropping her gaze from his. His open admiration surprised her. It had been a long time since she'd been with a man whose intent was to make her feel special, even desirable. That definitely wasn't Paul's intent. He belittled her at every turn. "There you go again comparing the two." She scolded herself inwardly.

Aleeya hated that she kept comparing Jenus to Paul, but she couldn't help it. She knew her relationship with Paul had fizzled long before the fateful night that ended everything. She hadn't felt goosebumps or sparks in a long time; those had stopped flying between them long before they ever broke it off. But Jenus's attentiveness was quenching a dry place deep in her soul. Suffced to say, it felt good... deliciously good.

"You better watch yourself, Mr. Ballard. All of this charm could get you into trouble." She flirted.

"Yeah...little girlie, you better watch yourself! Don't make me come back down there," her mother's voice warned. *"And stop slouching!"*

Aleeya immediately straightened her slouching posture, then timidly looked at Jenus, who was giving her an engaging smile.

Clearing her throat, she bowed her head again, trying her best not to get lost in those smoldering green eyes of his. The road back from Paul hadn't been an easy one. The truth be told, she still didn't feel completely ready to get back into the swing of things like her family wanted her to, and she definitely wasn't prepared to add men to the mix. Men were a mystery that wasn't easily solved. One minute they could be Dr. Jekyll, the next the dreaded Mr. Hyde. They said one thing and did another. Act as they love you, then disappear on you. Whether they were Christian or not, in her opinion, they all had traits of Jekyll and Hyde. As handsome and good-hearted as Jenus appeared to be, she was sure that lurking somewhere close to the surface was a dark side that only time would reveal.

"So, tell me about yourself." He smiled as he finished off the last of his beverage.

Jolted out of her thoughts by his voice, Aleeya turned towards him gave him a roguish smile before speaking. "That could be a very in-depth conversation, Jenus. Are you sure you want to know?"

"Again, with the flirting...girl, I'm coming down there...." Betty's voice echoed in her ear.

"Just kidding," Aleeya quickly added, looking around, hoping not to see her mother's face.

"I like danger, and I like you, so I guess I'm willing to risk it." Jenus gave a rueful grin revealing those deep dimples.

A thought popped into her mind. How would a man deal with a woman being totally open and honest with him about herself? None of the little games people play when trying to cover up their bad stuff. Why of all nights she thought to do this, she didn't know. Maybe there was something in the tiny jazz club's hazy atmosphere or maybe she was just tired of the cat and mouse game most of her dates consisted of. Whatever the reason, tonight she decided to take a chance and do something different.

"I'll make a deal with you, Jenus. For one night only, I will be open and honest and tell you whatever you want to know regarding any two things about me...so choose wisely," Aleeya said, leaning forward just a little as Jenus quietly pondered what she had offered.

"Okay, question number one." He paused. "Are you ready?" he said, raising an eyebrow.

"Fire away!" Aleeya said calmly poised in her seat, never batting an eyelash.

"Has the man who's broke your heart been at our table tonight?" He said with a probing glare.

Aleeya drew back, clearly blindsided by his perceptive inquiry. "That's quite a question...what did you say your profession was again?" Aleeya chuckled nervously. She wasn't prepared for the deep waters yet.

"Um-hum...Cute and perceptive...all right now...go Jesus." Aleeya thought she could hear her mother cheer.

"I didn't say...and that's not an answer." His tone was warm but firm. His eyes never left hers.

"Okay...what makes you think I have an ex and am suffering from a broken heart?" Aleeya countered.

"Well, when a woman's been loved correctly, she has a glow about her that comes from being whole. But when it's been broken, that shimmer that should be there isn't."

"Ahhh...I see," Aleeya said timorously, realizing that he was indeed seeing something that all her makeup and clothing couldn't hide.

"I saw a hint of your glow this morning, but for some reason, it's not here tonight. I also know my gender. And for your glow to be in this state, you must have been dealing with one needy greedy idiot," he said in a matter-a-fact tone that caused her to smile. "So, with that said, has that man been at our table tonight?"

Aleeya sighed heavily and laid her drink on the table. *Open and honest,* she reminded herself. "Okay, I'll level with you. Yes, he has. I find that in some ways, he'd never far off. Maybe it's because I thought we were building something together, but the moment we hit a rough patch, he just up and disappeared on me without hesitation." She didn't know why the truth came pouring out like a waterfall, but it had.

"It's difficult to process how someone can love you one minute and then be gone the next. Not because they've died but because they decided to be done with you." For a moment, Aleeya was lost in her own thoughts before returning her eyes to his steady gaze. "Hum...so there you have it! I've definitely had my share of bruising, but thank God I'm not broken." She raised her glass to him and finished her drink.

"Well, you're in good company. I think all of us have gone through times of bruising and in some cases brokenness, but God knows how to both heal and use broken people as long as he is the glue holding the broken pieces together."

"From your lips to God's ears," she murmured.

"Now for my second question, and then afterward we dance...okay!"

"O-okay!" Aleeya hesitated for a moment. Feeling in some way, she had outsmarted herself. Jenus was by no means superficial and, with his one question, had blown Paul and all the other men she'd dated out the water. He was ripping through her defensives as quickly as her little Yorkie, Bosco, ripped up her morning newspaper. She needed to be on guard because what she felt at the start of their evening was beginning to simmer.

"Tell me about your mom and dad," he said, raising his finger to one of the waitresses to come and refresh their drinks. Once the waitress left, Jenus turned his full attention back to her.

"My mom is...well, was great. She was my heart and best friend. She gave me her work ethic and taught me how to love life with all its faults, twists, and turns. She gave me her love for all things chocolate, especially chocolate chip cookies, and she taught me how to love God and family." Aleeya allowed her words to trail off as a hint of sadness in her voice crept in.

"How long has she been gone?"

"Forever!" Aleeya looked up from her glass and gave a weak smile, then shrugged her shoulder. "She's been with the Lord for seven years now."

He allowed his hand to cross the table's small distance and gently rested it on top of hers. "I'm sorry for your loss, Aleeya. The ache of losing a loved one only lessens with time...but how much no one knows."

"Um...Mother's Day still hurts, but I'm getting there," Aleeya said, her eyes focused on the hand that was still covering hers, causing warmth to spread up her arm and work its way to her heart.

"So, what about your dad. Is he still living?"

"I have no relationship with my biological father. He walked out on my mom a month before I was born, and we have never heard from him since. My parents never married, and his family wouldn't get involved. So, my mom gave me her last name and told me God was my father and that I'd never want for anything. She kept that promise," Aleeya said proudly, giving Jenus a genuine smile.

"She sounded like an extraordinary woman."

"Yeah...she was." Aleeya smiled, looking a little passed Jenus to see not only her mother standing in the distance but some of her uncles and aunts too. Her Uncle Pat gave her two thumbs up which made her bow her head with a smile. Clearing her throat, she turned her eyes toward Jenus.

"Now, with your mom gone, do you wish you had...you know, known your dad?"

"I'd tell you, but that's would take you over your two questions limit." Aleeya teased. "Besides, you promised me one more dance," Aleeya said, standing up effectively shutting down the question-and-answer segment of their date. She needed to lose herself in the music and bury all the stuff that Jenus questions unearthed.

"Okay...but how do I get the rest of my questions answered?" He asked, standing up and taking her hand.

"Maybe you'll have to wow me with some more of your fancy footwork," she said teasingly.

"Well, in that case, prepare to be wowed." He said ushering her to the dance floor.

Aleeya allowed Jenus to led the way. The ambiance of the small jazz club and the music playing washed over her, making her lose herself in the rhythm.

Jenus was a great dancer, which completely surprised her. He was six-foot-three inches, but the man had moves just like he did way back in his high school football playing days. She only wished she could say the same about herself. She always thought of herself to be tall, and lanky. Even though she filled out in all the right places, it still did nothing to help her uncoordinated frame. At five-eleven, she had the height, but not the skills to make it in sports, as a model or a ballerina.

Thank God she had the smarts, but that didn't help her now when dancing with a partner took some level of finesse.   At least Jenus didn't make her feel awkward about how uncoordinated she was. He was truly a gentleman. When a slow, more mellow tempo began to play, Jenus pulled her close. She happily went into his arms, falling in sync with the mood of the music and the slow swaying movements he was directing. She smiled as his chin rested perfectly on the crown of her head.

"Are you having fun?" He whispered just above her ear.

At the moment, Aleeya couldn't' distinguish who made the comment, her mother or Jenus. It really didn't matter because the answer was the same.

"Yeah…I'm having fun." She sighed with a smile closing her eyes, and allowed the eighth-grader insider her to live out her fantasy while the woman she was for the moment began dreaming again.

Chapter Five

"A man's gift opens doors for him, and brings him before great men." Proverbs, 18:16

"Lord, I thank you." Aleeya blew a sigh of relief. This was her final presentation for the conferences, and her room was packed. She was thrilled that the hard work in developing her troubled youth program had gotten such a tremendous response. Many who listened to the presentation were interested in her coming to their organization to do a presentation. She was really beginning to see the Lord's plans take shape for her life.

"Ms. Thomas, I just have to say how very much I enjoyed your presentation this morning."

Startled by the strange male tenor behind her, Aleeya quickly looked up. Her eyes went wide with excitement at the attractive man standing behind her. "Ben Rawlins? Of all the people. Never in a million years would I think I'd run into you here," she gushed, holding out her arms to receive her old classmate's warm embrace. "What in the world are you doing here?"

"Being blown away by your presentation, Artie." Benjamin Rawlins pulled her in for another quick hug. Then pulled away admirably and smiled. "Wow, you're just as stunning as ever."

"And you're still a big ole flirt." She admonished. "Okay, hands...let me see them." She ordered with a smirk. He smiled as he proudly displayed both ringless hands.

"Okay, let me see yours...Artie." He commanded, of which she complied, showing off her bare fingers. Pulling her ring finger closer to his face, he gave a thorough inspection, making her laugh. "I'm checking for tan lines because there's no way your still not married."

"Get out of here." She playfully shoved him away, then momentarily looked at him. He hadn't changed all that much. He was the classic cliché of tall, dark, and handsome that had her and a few others swooning over him all those years ago. But instead of dating back in high school, they just kept things on the friendship level. Looking at him now with his perfectly shaped bald head, milk chocolate skin tone, cleft chin, and deep dimples to boot, she had no idea what possessed her to do such a foolish thing. He left for college right after graduation and rarely came back to Jericho. For several years, she thought about him about what could've been, then she met Paul and quickly those thoughts went out the window.

"Wow, I can't believe you're here," she said softly. "But more than that, I can't believe you're not married. No one has snagged you up?"

"Me? What about you? Ms. Homecoming Queen of Jericho High and most likely to succeed at everything."

"Stop it!" She chuckled. "Besides my number one pick, that handsome quarterback that walked me down the field, you remember him? Hum…what's his name?" she said sarcastically. "Well, last I heard, he got a scholarship and never gave me or Jericho a backward glance." she countered.

Ben puckered his lips, "Yeah…yeah, that's your story, but as I recall, it was you who wouldn't give me the time of day!"

"Yeah, right… I'm sticking with my version of the story." They both laughed.

He looked at her admirably, then shook his head. "Wow…it's hard to believe that was nearly twenty years ago," Ben said. "Have you been back home…to Jericho?"

"I was there for a while before I left. Mom was really the only person keeping me there. Once she passed, I just didn't see a reason to remain." Aleeya decided he didn't need to know the gory details of why she left, including the failed engagement.

"Yeah, your mom was the best. She was your biggest cheerleader back then. I know she must be looking down on you now with nothing but pride."

"I hope so. I miss her a lot," Aleeya said, looking beyond Ben's head to see her mom standing in the distance, giving her an exaggerated wink. Aleeya blew out a slow breath and then refocused on Ben. "I guess that was one of the main reasons I haven't been back there as of late, too many memories." She smiled. "So, what about you? Have you been back to the old neighborhood?"

"Well, believe it or not, I returned to Jericho about two and a half years ago."

"Seriously, you returned? Why?!" she gave him an incredulous glare.

"It's a long story that I'd love to share with you over lunch if you're interested?"

A flutter began bouncing around in her stomach. It was definitely not the same feeling she had when she was with Jenus. It was the God type of flutter telling her this was not a by chance encounter. Jenus would be in presentations all day, so a bite to eat with her former classmate wouldn't interfere with their evening plans. "Okay, Mr. Rawlins, I'm interested," she said, picking up her final bag and automatically handed it to the hand he extended.

An hour later, Aleeya and Ben sat at a quaint little outdoor café, deep in conversation discussing life after college, where they had traveled, and the lessons they'd learned along the way. Aleeya had forgotten how animated Ben could be when just talking about life. But his genuine passion was his work with troubled youth, a passion they both shared.

"Aleeya, your program is just what we need to help bridge the gap between what we do at Eagle Crest Academy and the parents," he insisted.

A phone call interrupted their conversation, so he stepped away to take it, giving her a moment to seriously think about what he was offering her. He didn't want any ole program; he wanted her program to be implemented personally for all Eagle Crest Academy group homes nationwide.

Her heartbeat fluttered with excitement as she rehearsed his words in her head. *"You'll have a chance to oversee your program from the ground up!"*

The offer was more than alluring; it was a dream come true. She would have something of her own to implement as she saw fit. There was a fly in the ointment, though, the one thing about the opportunity that made her heart sink.

"You'd have to return to Jericho," Ben had indicated. "Jericho's facility is home base, so everything will need to start from there and branch out."

So, this once and a lifetime opportunity came with one significant string. She'd have to return to the one place on earth she detested…Jericho.

Sighing heavy, she instinctively wrapped her arms around her waist, stretching her fingers in search of that familiar protrusion under her clothing. That scar was her reminder. It would never let her forget how bad things got in Jericho and why she never considered returning...until now.

"You got to let go of the past to grab hold of your future, honey." The gentle words of her mother surfaced in her heart. Aleeya looked around to see if her mother had popped up, but Betty was nowhere in sight.

"Sorry about that Artie, I had to strong-arm one of my presenters into covering for me."

"Oh, my goodness, Ben, I'm so sorry, I didn't realize you had to do a presentation," Aleeya stated, frantically picking up her purse and reaching for her belongings.

"Stop that. I covered for my team member earlier this week now he can return the favor. Besides, you're not getting out of here without telling me your life story, especially why any sensible man hasn't made you, his bride."

"Maybe it's because I've never been able to get over the one that slipped through my fingers." Aleeya looked at him craftily.

"Oh, please!" he rolled his eyes, breaking into laughter.

"And what about you? There is no way in the world you should be sitting across from me ringless. I know of at least a dozen girls who wanted you back in the day, if memory serves me correctly."

"Yeah, well, for all I know half of those girls your thinking of could either be my half-sister or first cousin." He snickered. "Heck, for all I know, you could be my half-sister as much as my dad played around." Ben chuckled, but the smile never reached his face.

Aleeya never knew who her father was, but Ben knew his father all too well. It was one of the reasons she and Ben decided to just be friends, for fear that down the line, they'd discover they were kissing cousins...for real. It was well known in Jericho that the Rawlins' men got around. Mr. Ben Rawlins Sr. and his three other brothers were infamous for their womanizing and cheating ways. Ben seemed to be passed this painful place in his life from what Aleeya could see, so maybe there was hope for her yet.

"Hey since I'm free this afternoon, why don't you ditch the rest of the conference and take a ride with me so we can see the sights of this beautiful island? That way, I can have all the time in the world to convince you to come back home and work with me at Jericho."

Aleeya was about to say no. She had plans with Jenus later, and didn't want to be too tired. But before she could decline, her phone buzzed. It was a text from him.

"Hello, beautiful. I hate doing this to you, but one of my guys cut out on me, so I need to cover for him this evening, which will ruin our dinner plans. I hate not seeing you tonight, but I'd love it if you'd allow me to make it up to you tomorrow, just you and me. I promise it will be special."

"I hope everything is all right?" Ben inquired.

"Everything is fine, and a drive touring this lovely island with you sounds wonderful," she said, smiling, although, in her heart, she was disappointed not seeing Jenus that evening. She planned on texting him just that, along with his need to make their day tomorrow extra...extra special.

Chapter Six

"To whom much is given much is required." Luke 12:48

Jenus looked out at the panoramic view of the ocean the conference room within the hotel offered. The tinted windows open partially so those inside could still feel and smell the breeze from the ocean air. The room itself was state of the art featuring white boards, drop down video screens and surround sound. But as innovative as it was, Jenus longed to be out walking the beach with Aleeya at his side. Last night he had an amazing time. They dance, talked and laughed the night away. If only Ben hadn't requested this impromptu staff meeting effectively ruining his dinner plans with her for that evening. He was sure he could've gotten the rest of his questions about Aleeya answered. Tapping his pen on the table, Jenus immediately felt agitation as Ben strolled in the door.

"Hey Jenus, good to see you man. By the way thanks for covering for me this afternoon." Ben smiled patting Jenus on the back.

"That's what team members do for each other. Besides, it's not like you haven't covered for me from time to time." Jenus cordially responded.

"I realize that and trust me, it was greatly appreciated, but I know it was last minute, so I hope I didn't ruin any dancing plans you had for the evening." He smirked.

"What is that supposed to mean?" Jenus said with a raised eyebrow. Admittedly, Ben wasn't his favorite person in the world. The man was a politician who always had some type of an agenda. Of course, no one else on the team saw it that way, so he kept his opinion about the guy to himself.

"Oh, nothing," Ben said casually, walking slightly away. "It was just....well, the team decided to check out that jazz place you raved about last year. So, we all went last night and were surprised to see you dancing the night away with...hum, who was that beautiful woman you were with?"

"She's my business and none of yours," Jenus stared him down.

Raising both his hands in surrender, Ben shrugged a shoulder. "No need to get touchy. I was just hoping that my abrupt change of plans; this afternoon didn't put you in a bind with her."

"It didn't." Jenus lied. He turned his back on Ben to regaining his composure knowing full well Ben's absence that afternoon and now this spontaneous meeting had altered Jenus plans to see Aleeya. As other Eagle Crest team members began filling the conference room, Jenus fought to get his head on straight. The only solace he had was the text message Aleeya left him.

"My day will not be as bright without seeing your handsome face. You better make tomorrow extra special for me, Mr. Ballard!" Artie.

"So is that a text from the mystery girl we saw you dancing the night away with, Jenie." A woman's voice spoke from behind.

Jenus rolled his eyes. Of all the people who had to see him that night, it would be his best friends' wife, Acsah Benford, Ace, as she was affectionally called by everyone. Jenus decided to keep his mouth shut.

"Oh, so it's like that. You don't want to talk about your mystery woman, then she must be extra special." Ace placed her arms around his shoulders and teased. "Jenie's got a girlfriend."

"Neil, come get your wife." Jenus turned toward his friend Othniel Benford for rescue.

"Ace!" Othniel warned.

Sucking her teeth, Acsah walked into her husband's open arms, stood on tippy-toes, and kissed his chin. "You two are no fun at all…well, that is unless one of the two of you are trying to do the salsa." Ace mockingly did a dance, then yelped when her husband friskily slapped her derriere.

"Behave, woman." Neil playfully tweaked her nose, then shook hands with Jenus. "Although I have to say, it was refreshing to see you out enjoying yourself last night."

"That's all I was saying." Ace spoke up with a frown.

"Yeah, but it's the way you say it, dear." He eyed his wife and was rewarded with her spiritedly sticking out her tongue at him before scurrying out of his reach.

"How about we stop talking about my nightlife and get on with this meeting," Jenus grumbled.

"Agreed," Ace chimed in. "That way, I'll have more time to post the video I took last night of Jenie dancing. I'm sure the ladies back in Jericho would love to see it."

"Ace!" both Neil and Jenus spoke at the same time.

"Touchy...touchy!" She smirked.

"That's what I said. Very touchy indeed. Must have a thing for this no-named woman he was with." Ben spoke up from across the room.

Something about Ben's demeanor was rubbing Jenus the wrong way. The man had a look about him that said he knew something the rest of them didn't. "Like I said can we get down to business." Jenus tone effectively squashed any further comments from his team.

"Absolutely." Ben said turning on the smart screen. In a few seconds, Joshua Cobbs and Caleb Bell faces appeared. "I would say good evening, but I know where you guys are its right in the middle of the night so let's get started, shall we?"

"Josh, Caleb... It's good to see you. Forgive our appearance, but we weren't made aware this meeting was going to be with the entire board." Jenus said with an edge in his tone feeling a little uncomfortable wearing shorts, a tee-shirt, and flip flops. He hated being out of the loop, which lately was a lot.

"That's my fault, Jenus, and I do apologize for again the short notice. But I have good news, and I wanted to share it with everyone before I leave out tomorrow," Ben interjected.

Jenus conceded and took his seat but still felt a little on edge. Ben always had something up his sleeve.

"The reason I called this meeting is that there are going to be a few changes on the horizon for Eagle Crest Academy at Jericho, good changes that I need you guys to be prepared for."

"Changes like...?" Jenus calm demeanor didn't reflect the twisting and knotting of his gut.

"The state has accepted our proposal. We are going to be fully funded to operate as a residential treatment facility and can start taking new kids in as soon as this coming September."

"Woohoo...that's excellent!" Ace cheered.

"Wow, I can't believe it. This is great," Othneil chimed in.

Jenus remained quiet as many board members congratulated and asked questions about how quickly they could get moving. Something was eating at him. He couldn't say precisely what but knew it was something.

"Jenus, don't you have anything you want to say?" Othniel asked.

"Yeah, I do." Jenus sat up in his seat. "Jakob Gains is currently acting director at Jericho. Still, he lacks the experience and credentials needed to be a director of a residential treatment facility. September is only nine months away." With that said Jenus turned his chair to face Ben. "Ben, is that really enough time to find and hire a director, hire and train additional staff, while simultaneously recruiting kids for this program?" Jenus asked. Many of the board members in the meeting were nodding their heads in support of the concerns Jenus raised. Feeling their backing Jenus continued.

"Who have you assigned to take on this responsibility, because whoever it is needs to be seriously qualified to manage such a huge undertaking?" Jenus admonished. The room remained quiet...too quiet. As realization began to overshadow him, the twisting in his gut tightened. He was the fatted calf being led to the slaughter. He was the one Ben had in mind to direct the academy back in Jericho.

Chapter Seven

"Get rid of all bitterness, rage, and anger, brawling and slander, along with every form of malice."
Ephesians 4:31-32

There was a sweet smell lingering in the night air that was soothing to the soul. Aleeya couldn't detect what was causing the fragrance, but the pleasant scent tickled her nose. The night air was not too cool for a wrap, just warm enough to enjoy the outdoor events hosted by the resort. There was the distinct sound of a ukulele being played in the background as the live band performed their first set. Aleeya breathed in and then out, allowing the tension in her neck to fade away. She hadn't had flashbacks of the night of her assault in years. It was her sign that she was getting better and allowing the past to be just that, the past. So, it had to be her conversation about returning to Jericho that afternoon with Ben that caused the horrible memories to resurface. The attack was brutal, and her attacker was vicious. The events of that night played out like a scene in a movie.

Every person played a role in what happened that day, including Paul, who wasn't even physically there. As the anger grew in her soul, she tightly twisted her long thin braids around her finger, almost cutting off the circulation.

"Breathe, Aleeya, just breathe," her heart whispered.

Inhaling deeply, she slowly released the trapped air in her lungs. As the anger for the people, she saw in that room began to surface, she prayed in her heart. "I forgive them, Lord, I truly forgive them." Then an image of Terry Kincaid with his drunken face came into view. With every offensive slur he belted out, he gave a vicious kick in her side. She winced and placed her hand on her side. The pain was no longer there but, her mind felt every humiliating blow.

"This, too, needs to be forgiven," a gentle whisper implored.

Her heart hammered in her chest. She watched helplessly as her mind replayed how her precious gift of life was being bludgeoned to death by this mad man's steel-toed boot. He didn't care for his own family and now mercilessly took life from her. "But father, he robbed me!" Aleeya vehemently spoke into the night air.

"Daughter, as long as you don't forgive, you are allowing him to rob you of your peace, joy, and healing."

She hadn't thought of it in those terms. Blinded by her sorrow of what could have been, she hadn't really focused on her here and now.

"You can't forgive what you are unwilling to relinquish to the father," the spirit whispered.

Taking a deep breath, knowing this was way past due, she closed her eyes and said the words, "Lord, I forgive him." Immediately what felt like a warm blanket to a wet, shivering body, peace and comfort enveloped her mind and gave her rest deep within. As the tension in her shoulders lessened and the tightness in her chest lifted, she blew out a very long, weighty sigh. She had a decision to make. Thinking about the past wouldn't help her move forward in her future. The naive social worker who had walked into a volatile situation totally unprepared for what came next was gone. She had changed for the better, but still, was she really ready to return home to Jericho? She had spent five years doing the opposite, running from the place that had wounded her in every way imaginable. Even now, with all her gains, was she strong enough?

"With God, all things are possible if you believe."

It was her mother's favorite scripture; one she had come to love over the years as well. Bowing her head, she laced her fingers together and did the only thing she knew for sure would give her the correct answer. Closing her eyes, she prayed. "Lord, search my heart. You know why I feel anxious, but you also know what's the best path for me to take. Please speak to me tonight and let me know which direction I should take in Jesus's name. Amen!"

"Amen from me as well," came a deep tenor from over her head.

Startled by the intrusion in her quiet time with God, Aleeya jolted upright, then immediately relaxed, smiling up at Jenus. "Hey, stranger."

"Hey yourself," Jenus said, leaning over and giving her a gentle peck on the forehead.

She placed her hand on his cheek and spontaneously kissed the other side. "I wasn't expecting to see you at all today, but I'm so happy you're here."

"Likewise, beautiful." He took the back of her hand and gently caressed it with his lips. "I was just about to take a walk on the beach and happened to see you sitting over here. I just couldn't let the opportunity of seeing my favorite person on the island go, and I'm glad I did. You look troubled...is everything all right?" He asked, taking a seat next to her and placed his arm around her shoulder.

Instinctively she snuggled up beside him resting her head on his shoulder. "Things just got a whole lot better now that you're here," she surprisingly confessed.

"You sweet talker. Keep saying things like that, and you might find yourself getting kissed before the night is over." He chuckled.

"You might find yourself being kissed right back and more than once." She winked, then playfully puckered her lips.

"You're going to mess up my Christian witness, little lady." He raised his eyebrow toward her.

"Nah! I love God too much to do that, although I've heard that God is forgiving," she said brazenly, batting her eyelashes.

"Let's go," he said, pulling her up from her seat and onto her feet.

"Hey, where are we going." Aleeya laughed, holding on to his hand as he quickly led them toward the closest pier on the beach.

"I'm going to re-baptize you in this ocean because you need Jesus."

"Did you say I need Jesus or Jenus? Cause I'm very fond of them both, you know...especially the one who threatened to kiss me," she said, laughing until he scooped her up in his arms, kicked off his sandals, and walked just at the water's edge. Screeching, she held on to Jenus tight. "What are you doing?" she screamed again as he looked as if he was lowering her in the water.

"If you don't behave, I'm going to throw you in," he playfully threatened while allowing the water to splash over his legs.

"You wouldn't dare." She then screeched with wide-eyed surprise as she felt him lowering her toward the water. "Jenie, no, don't. Okay...okay, I promise, I'll behave." She tittered.

"You better," he said softly. "Now, take your shoes off."

"Look at you trying to get me undressed already, and it's only our second date." She tsked giving him a scolding look.

"Very funny. However, if you'd rather me just plop your sandal-clad feet in this water, I'd be happy too," he said while lowering her feet toward the water again.

"If you do, I'll kiss you for sure." She wrapped her arms around his neck and moved her head within inches of his.

"That promise will definitely get your feet wet, Ms. Thomas."

"Well, in that case, let me give you a sample of what you're in for." Aleeya boldly announced before ever so gently kissing him tenderly on the lips. She wasn't the bold type and had never made the first move with any man in her entire life, but this thing between her and Jenus was fun and exciting. Maybe she was so relaxed with him because he made her feel safe and protected. Perhaps it was just because he was her junior high crush, and she was living out some type of romantic fantasy in paradise. Whatever the reason, she was grateful and definitely felt it was worth her doing something as bold as kissing him.

It had to be one of the sweetest kisses she ever had, and she didn't want it to end. She'd have gladly continued if not for the sudden feeling of her feet being plunged into the cold water of the Pacific. Popping her eyes open in surprise, she laughed in disbelief. "Agh! Jenus, you stinker." Looking down at her soaking wet feet, then back up to his sheepish grin, on impulse, Aleeya kicked her feet up, splashing his legs, shorts, and shirt with ocean water. She then quickly tried to escape his grasp by running in the opposite direction.

Laughing, Jenus apprehended her by the waist with ease. "Oh no, you don't, Ms. Thomas." His rich vibrato rumbled over her head as he lifted her off her feet and brought their foreheads together. "That's not the punishment you promised me."

Smiling up at him, she stared into the tender glow in his eyes that reflected his gentle soul. She didn't know or understand the strange connection they had, but right now wasn't the time to explore it.

"Well, I guess I wouldn't be truthful if I didn't keep my word to you," she said, standing on her tiptoes to rub her nose with his.

"I sure would hate to report to the powers that be that you're not a woman of your word." Jenus admonished.

"That would be just awful," she said, liking the way his breath felt on her lips. "My word wouldn't be worth anything if I don't do what I say." She said, loving his closeness.

"So, I guess the only decent and honest thing for you to do is…punish me." He wiggled his eyebrows.

Feeling his arms tightening around her waist, she wouldn't argue the right and wrong of kissing this man she wasn't in a relationship with. Right now, all she wanted to do was issue out Jenus' punishment in the most creative ways she could imagine.

Chapter Eight

"For I know the plans that I have for you, declares the Lord…" Jeremiah 29:11

Going to bed that night, Aleeya could not dislodge the smile on her face. She found herself waking up early that morning, still smiling about the extensive punishment she doled out to Jenus that night. True to form, he pulled away before things became too intense and suggested they take a walk. Knowing they both needed to cool down, she held the hand he offered her as they walked in companionable silence down the sandy shore, then found a dry spot to sit. They discussed life and how good God had been to them over the years. She wanted to tell him about her life in Jericho, even the not-so-good parts. However, things were going so well between them; why spoil it with a serious conversation like that?

She didn't know how late it was when he walked her to her hotel room, but by that time, her boldness had ended, and her common sense had returned. His must-have, too, as all he did was lean in, gave her nose a quick peck, and promised to see her tomorrow. With that, he opened her hotel door, gently pushed her inside, and shut her in.

Her feistiness hadn't completely died, though, as she quickly thought of something to entice him to come in for a little while, but when she opened the door and looked down the hallway, it was empty. "Thanks, Lord," she said, pulling her head back into the room, knowing that God was definitely her keeper that night.

In the silence of her darkened room, Aleeya looked at the shadows dancing off the walls, remembering a time when her evening wouldn't have wrapped up so nicely. If she had been with Paul, they both would have been repenting. A queasy feeling began rumbling in her gut as past memories of their time together surfaced. "No...no...no!" she spoke out, pounding her fist on the top covers and rolling her head from side to side. She didn't want to ruin such a lovely night thinking of her past failed relationship with Paul. He was a jerk and a deceiver. God had spared her a lifetime of pain dealing with his dumb...Aleeya sighed deeply and purposely bit her tongue to keep from cursing. "Father, I walk in forgiveness with Paul. He is your child, and therefore I leave him in your hands. Amen!" She blew out a breath.

She hadn't had to pray that prayer in a long time. Shutting her eyes, she would try and get a little more sleep when her cell phone began to ring. Jumping up quickly, she automatically reached for it off her nightstand. Looking at the caller ID, she smiled and fell back on her pillow to answer Jordin's call. Clicking over, she greeted her longtime friend.

"Hello, sister-friend, what is it that I can do for you at four in the morning?"

"It is not my fault that while the rest of the world is starting their day, those living in paradise are still in bed." Jordin chuckled. "Besides, I did call you at a decent time last night, but you were nowhere to be found...hum, not having some little romantic trysts, are you...if so, I want details," she said with excitement.

"I plead the fifth, now what are you calling me for? I was just about to drift off to sleep again."

"Oh, so you were awake, hum...was there a certain special someone running through your mind keeping you up last night?" She pressed.

"Pleading the fifth...remember."

"Awe...come on, Artie, you've got to give me something. Here I am stuck in Jericho, where it's cold and snowy, and you're living it up in sunny, balmy Hawaii," Jordin complained.

"Yeah...well, no one told you and Jess to get pregnant sooner than you were supposed to. Now, if you two had the good sense to get pregnant after the trip, well, you wouldn't have to wonder what I'm doing because you'd be here to see it." She chuckled.

"Yada...yada...yada," Jordan mocked. "Fine, be that way. I guess I'll have to get my information from other sources," she said mysteriously.

"What other sources?"

"Now I'm pleading the fifth." Jordin mocked.

"Whatever, there is nothing to tell." She winced. She wasn't completely candid with her but had her reasons. Besides, what was she supposed to say? In the last two days, she met a man she became wildly attracted to on the first date and made out with him at midnight on the second date? She already knew what would come next. *"Aleeya Rochelle Thomas, have you lost your mind!"* Yeah, she had. There was no need for her best friend to confirm what she already knew.

"Okay, so if you don't want to talk pleasure, let's talk business. So, I'm told you have something that Eagle Crest Academy can't do without," Jordin said cryptically.

"Jordi, what in the world are you talking about?" Aleeya furrowed her eyebrows with the question.

"I'm talking about the little chat you had with a certain Benjamin Rawlins."

"Ben, how do you know him?" Aleeya was mystified

"You do remember that Jericho is a small town, where everyone knows everyone," Jordin chuckled.

"Right." Aleeya shook her head remembering how hard it was to keep your business private in town like Jericho. Just one more reason for not wanting to return. "Wow, news travels fast. Yeah, I ran into Ben today. We discussed at length the possibility of running my program at his facility.... But why would that interest you?"

"His facility is connected to my counseling agency. We do all of the counseling for the academy. So, if you do take his offer, you know what that means?"

"What?"

"We'd be working together again. Oh, Aleeya, just think of it. You and me together again in Jericho... I would be thrilled."

Aleeya could hear the emotion in her friend's voice. Yes, she would love to work with Jordi again if it were any place but Jericho. "Yeah, it would be a bonus to work with you again," Aleeya confessed.

"Yeah, and this time we wouldn't have to worry about being thrown into crazy situations like before. Which is definitely a perk when running your own business. I am so thankful that God and Jess pushed me to do this... it's been such a blessing."

"It sounds like your dreams are finally coming true. I'm so happy for you, Jordi. I truly am."

"It's time for some of your dreams to manifest, too Artie. I know the state of mind you were in when you left Jericho, and I know how hard it is for you to even consider coming back...but I just feel there is something here for you. I believe God wants to turn things around in your favor."

"Look, I won't deny it. God has been talking to me for some time about come back home. Although I love living in Florida, and I can see myself making a living out there, I've always had that tug of returning to Jericho. When I saw Ben today, and we started talking about the possibilities of my future, I must admit it got my curiosity up."

"Oh Artie, that's wonderful. You can stay with Jess and me until you get your own place, and then we can...."

"Whoa...whoa, slow down, let me finish. As great as everything sounds, I gotta be honest, I'm scared. Just talking about the possibly of me returning to Jericho gave me flashbacks of that awful night." Aleeya shuttered with her head held between her hands. "I don't know if I'm strong enough to deal with all of that again."

Jordin listened and then interjected. "Artie, what happened to you is no small matter. Having flashbacks of something so traumatic is not only understandable, but it's actually normal. It takes God and time to fully heal."

"Jordi, I know your right about that, but...I just don't know." Aleeya sighed, holding her hand over her forehead. "It's just that, back then, I felt there was this higher purpose or call, if you will, for my life. So, I went hard pursuing my call to counsel others, trying to save the world, one family at a time. Then I came up against the Kincaid's, got the crap kicked out of me, and barely survived." Aleeya paused for a moment, trying to clear her head of the memories while articulating what she was trying to convey. "I guess after everything that has happened and having time to reflect, I'm not the same person. I don't feel like saving the world anymore."

Feeling both free and ashamed of her confession, Aleeya allowed her penned-up tears to flow.

"Artie, I wish I had a magic wand that could heal your heart, mend all the broken and shattered pieces of your soul, but only God can heal us fully. In Matthews eleven verse twenty-eight, it says, *'Come unto me all you who are weak and heavy laden, and I will give you rest. Take my yoke on you and learn of Me'*. Let me ask you this question, Aleeya, are you allowing the Lord to deal with the trauma of your soul?"

"No," she silently confessed.

"Why?"

"Because it's God's fault," Aleeya blurted out, then burst into tears with the admittance.

"Why, Jordi, did it have to happen at all? Why me? All I was doing was trying to help them, and Terry beat me like I wasn't even a person...he literally kicked the life out of me." Aleeya stopped herself from saying more. Although they were close friends, she hadn't revealed to Jordi that she was pregnant with Paul's child the night of her attack. No one knew she had lost the baby other than her doctors.

"Artie, have you confessed to God that you're angry with him?"

"What will it change? What happened... happened." Swiping at the few tears that trickled down her cheeks, Aleeya exhaled before speaking. "Anyway, it was a long time ago. I'm tired of being mad. I just want to live free and enjoy life."

"I know you want to be free of it, so just remember this. Who Jesus sets free is free indeed.
You feel free because you're away from Jericho and not facing the situation. But the true freedom Christ gives will allow you to stare the problem in the face, and it won't bother you anymore. You'll remember what happened, but the pain and trauma of it wouldn't cling to you anymore. That's true freedom Artie, please don't settle for less. Hey listen, I gotta go into a counseling session, but Artie, think about what I said, okay?"

"Okay...I will. Aloha Jordi and mahalo."

"Mahalo...what does that mean?"

"Thanks!"

Chapter Nine

"Behold I do a new thing: now it shall spring forth; shall ye not know it?" Isaiah 43:19

"Paddle boarding? You're taking me paddle boarding?" Aleeya eyed Jenus suspiciously as they sped down the highway coast. It wasn't long after Aleeya hung up that morning with Jordi that her hotel room phone rang. Jenus voice was still raspy with sleep but still gave her goosebumps when he said, good morning, brown eyes. His instructions were simple, wear shorts and a bathing suit and meet him in the lobby in one hour. When she got to the entrance, there he stood, looking amazingly rugged in his khaki cargo shorts and green sleeveless tee that accentuated his brawny arms. When she inquired about where they were going, all he'd say was, it's a surprise. Good thing he didn't tell her.

"For the fifth time, yes, Artie, we are going paddle boarding this morning." He grinned, staring sideways at her.

"Well, where are the paddleboards? I don't see anything in this vehicle that remotely looks like paddleboards?"

"They're right there in the back." He pointed in the back of his truck.

"What those bright yellow fold-up things.?" she asked in wide-eyed astonishment. "That looks more like a fold-up chair than a paddleboard.

"It's an Origamipaddler, and yes, before you even ask, they are absolutely safe on the water."

"Humph…so you say."

"Yes, I say. I've been using this board since I got here… haven't had a mishap once."

"Okay, look, Jenus, you do recognize that no matter how light my complexion is, I am, I'm still a black woman with braids in her hair. Seeing that under that tan of yours, you appear to be a brotha, so I'm sure you're aware of our hair issues?"

"Oh, come on, city girl, nothing is gonna happen to your braids," he said, reaching out and taking one of the long coils between his fingers and giving a gentle tug. "Besides, where's your sense of adventure?" He admonished. "Where did that free-spirited woman from last night go?"

"She took a very long moderately cold shower and came to her senses." She smirked.

"Yeah, well, mine was much longer than yours and definitely cold." Turning sideways to look at her, he confessed. "By the way, your punishment nearly did me in last night. I had to run the steps to keep from coming back to your door," he confessed.

"So that's how you disappeared so quickly. It's a good thing you did. That free-spirited person you met the other night might have done something that would've messed both of our Christian witnesses up, which is why I have Artie on lockdown. So, the only one you're going to deal with today is sensible, level-headed Aleeya."

"Okay, I can deal with sensible Aleeya, but you've got to let go a little. Let a bit of the Artie in you out so you can have fun on our date. Besides, this is my last day in paradise, and I want to spend every moment of it with you."

His confession made her smile on the outside while her heart sank within. She knew this day was coming, the day they would need to say aloha to each other and get back to the reality of their individual lives.

She purposely wanted to keep things upbeat between them. Their time spent together had been fun and romantic. Everyone in life deserved that, didn't they? To have a little romance to cushion them from the hard times in-between? Aleeya looked out over the water where the sun was just breaking the crest of the blue ocean, signaling that morning was on the way.

" You're getting awfully quiet on me over there."

"I was just thinking that the sunrises over here are just as glorious as the sunsets, and how magnificent God is for creating them both." Aleeya quietly spoke.

"What does the scripture say? From the rising of the sun to the going down of the same, the Lord is truly worthy to be praised."

"That's in Psalms, I think," she said softly, then remained quiet before speaking again. "You know, sometimes I truly wonder, when I look at all the beauty of God's creation and how we have messed so much of it up, it makes you wonder why God bothers with us at all."

"It's His choice to love us. He knows everything about us, nothing is hidden. He knew what sin would do to this world, but he still allows us to make choices."

"Do you ever feel like you don't have a choice? That somehow your choice was taken from you?" Aleeya asked, noticing how Jenus knuckles gripped the steering wheel with the question.

"Yes, I have felt like that a couple of times in life," Jenus responded in an even tone.

"Well, how do you deal with that? I mean, I know the right answer is, God knows best. But sometimes it doesn't feel like it, especially when something you didn't want to give up is taken from you."

He remained silent for a moment, making her wish she had never opened this can of worms. They were having such a great time, and today was his last day here. She was about to say never mind when he spoke up.

"I lost someone significant to me a while back, not by my choice but by an unfortunate string of events that were out of my control. For the longest time, I questioned God about why he allowed it to happen. I was robbed, and I blamed God. I felt he was responsible for the loss I endured because he was able to stop it from happening."

"I can relate to what you're saying." Aleeya admitted, knowing how close to home Jenus was hitting with his own confession. "How did you get beyond feeling that way?"

"I'm not going to lie, there are times I still wonder why things turned out the way they did. Then I started to pray a prayer of surrender, and not just say I surrender, but really mean the words in my heart. I had to stop treating God as if he were my personal genie in a bottle. I'd only let him out when I wanted things, then stuffed him back in the bottle when I thought I could handle things independently. Of course, there's a lot more to the story, but I had a choice to make. I could continue to blame God or choose to make Him the solution to my problem."

"Make him the solution to your problems," Aleeya mumbled to herself.

"No, not problems...problem."

"Oh, I would love to say I only had one problem in life, but I have many issues that I need God to resolve."

"No, you don't, brown eyes." He looked at her then laughed at the incredulous look she was giving back to. him. "You have one problem...and you're it."

"Oh, so you're saying I'm the problem." She pointed to herself and laughed as he vigorously, nodding his head.

"You and everyone else on the planet. Hands down, we are our biggest problem, and God is the solution."

"Okay, how do you figure?" she lightheartedly challenged.

"Perfect example. We are going paddleboarding, but fear holds you back from having the best time of your life. When God is your solution, he won't allow you to run from fear; he'll cause you to face it."

"I'm not afraid of the paddleboard. It's falling off the paddleboard, into the ocean, and then sinking to the bottom that concerns me," she said in a matter-a-fact tone.

"Aleeya, I can guarantee you that you wouldn't sink to the bottom of the ocean floor."

"Oh really, how can you guarantee such a thing?"

"I'm sure sharks would eat you before you ever hit bottom." He chuckled then said, *ouch* after she punched him in the arm.

"You just played the wrong hand, buddy. Now I am definitely not going in. I don't care what you say!"

"We'll see about that," he said cryptically.

"Jenus Ballard, there is nothing you can do or say that is going to get me in the water on that thing," Aleeya said definitively. Occasionally she would glance out of the corner of her eye at him. Still, he kept driving smiling the entire time. "Why do you have that smirk on your face?" she questioned, unable to take his silence any longer.

"I have my reasons, city girl."

"Well, you don't know what city I'm from, so you better watch yourself," she said sassily, swaying her head from side to side.

"Um-hum."

"Okay, you've been warned." She crossed her arms and puckered her lips. "You're not the first man I've had to school, and you won't be the last."

"Really, Ms. Thomas?" He looked over at her with a doubtful expression.

"Oh, don't let my slender size fool you." She countered his look with a look of her own. "I know how to handle myself," she retorted confidently, knowing within herself how efficient she'd become in the self-defense classes she had taken for the past five years while in Florida. Not to brag on herself, but she had picked up quite a few moves.

As the car took the next turn, it slowed and went down a long windy road that opened up to the prettiest view she'd ever seen. They seemed to be surrounded by waterfalls, and the way the rising sun reflected off the water made it look like liquid gold. Aleeya was already unbuckling her seatbelt and pushing the door open. Kicking off her sandals, she ran toward the shoreline, and before she knew it, her feet were already in the water.

"Oh my God, Jenus, this place is breathtakingly beautiful," she gushed, looking up into the mist to see a vast rainbow encompassing one of the falls. She wished she had grabbed her cellphone out of the car so she could take a picture.

"Umm…what were you saying a few minutes ago about me not getting you into the water Ms. Thomas?" Jenus questioned as he came alongside her with his paddleboard resting in the water.

"You didn't get me in the water. I got in the water all by myself," Aleeya quibbled. Looking at him, he looked terrific in his black swim trunks. She was thankful they came down to his knees, already knowing she would likely have to repent for her wayward thoughts.

Remembering she was still in her shorts, she trotted back to the shore. She relinquished her shirt and shorts that hid her two-piece blue striped bathing suit that consisted of shorts and a sensible tank top. It was flattering to her shape but not too revealing. Stowing her things in the car, she hurried back with enthusiasm. "Okay, I'm ready for my first lesson."

"Good! How about we start with you learning how to get on this board?" He raised an eyebrow at her.

"That's easy!"

"It might look easy, but it may prove more of a challenge than you think."

"Maybe for you, but I got this." She wrinkled up her nose at him then looked down at the daunting task ahead of her. In her mind, getting on the board wasn't the issue. Staying balanced on the board was.

"Need a hand?" Jenus offered.

Shoving his extended hand away, she remarked, "No, thank you, I got this...augh!" No sooner than she said the words, her one foot that was on the board slid off, and she found herself barreling forward straight into Jenus rock-hard abs. "Ouch!" Her muffled voice spoke against his chest. Pulling back and rubbing her nose, her wet face looked into his laughing one. "What's in there, lead?" she said, poking him in the chest, clearly annoyed by her first unsuccessful attempt.

"No, nothing but hard work and discipline is in here, sweetheart." He patted his chest. "Although, I may need to have abs of steel to keep you upright on this board," he said, then he gingerly hopped up with both feet on the board with perfect balance.

"Show off." She sucked her teeth at him.

"Nah… that's all skill, baby." He jested, holding out his hand toward her.

"Aren't you afraid that I'll pull you in?"

"Nope…you're too much of a lady to do that sort of thing." He winked at her. "Now we can do this, one of two ways. You can climb onto the board belly first, then prop yourself up on your knees, or since you're a beginner, I can take you out on my board. That way, you can get the feel of things. Although you have this 'I'm woman, hear me roar' thing going on, I'm sure you wouldn't want that."

"On the contrary, Mr. Ballard, I would love for you to put those strong arms and abs to good use and ferry me across the ocean on your little um… what's this thing called again?" She squinted up at him.

"It's an origamipaddler." He with his mouth twisted in sarcasm.

"Yes, that's it, ferry me across the Pacific in my luxurious origamipaddler, kind sir." She stated in her most regal voice, waving toward the water as if she were queen of the Nile.

"Go and get a life preserver and then get on this paddleboard, woman!" He laughed at her antics.

Giggling, Aleeya ran back to the car, retrieved a life preserver, she then trotted back to the water while securing it in place. "Hey, what do I need this thing for anyway? I got you, don't I?"

"Yes, but safety is safety, and seeing you're accident-prone, I'd rather be safe than sorry."

She wrinkled her nose up at him for that wisecrack before saying, "You will be sorry if you tip us over. Definitely going to get a boatload of punishment for that." She winked.

"I'll keep that in mind," he said as he began paddling out in the water until it was waist-high. "Okay, now place your hands here on the board. Good, now push up until your belly is on the board. Good, now swing your feet over." He directed.

"Why can't I just get on my knees?"

"Because my way is easier."

"Says who?"

"Me, the one who knows what they're doing, that's who? Now let's go. Daylight is burning," he spoke.

"Okay, slave driver," Aleeya muttered, steadying herself with both hands. She then crawled on her belly until she was lying flat on the board then swung her feet around. "There, I did it without help," she said, proceeding to roll on her side, causing the board to tip sharply, flipping them both off the board. Screeching loudly, she splashed Jenus in the face when he emerged. "You did that on purpose."

"No, if I would've done it on purpose, you'd be the only one wet. Now come here, and I will show you how to get back on," he instructed.

Obediently, Aleeya swam toward him. Once in position on the board, he lifted her up by the waist until she was situated comfortably. Then, in one effortless motion, he climbed aboard and immediately stood. "So, you're going to teach me how to do all of what you just did...right."

"Remember, this is my last day in paradise, and from what I've seen, I'd need at least a week." He jested.

"Hey, I didn't do that bad." On impulse, she tickled the back of his calf, causing him to jerk his foot away, making the board yank in the opposite direction. Still, he quickly regained his balance before they capsized.

"You know, for a woman who doesn't like getting her hair wet, you sure like flirting with the possibility."

"Not true. I don't like flirting with the possibility of getting wet. I like flirting with the person I plan on giving the punishment to for getting me wet."

"Well, it seems the Artie from last night is beginning to make a surprise appearance."

"Oh…how do you know?"

"The Artie that I saw last night was definitely not shy around the fellas…or is it just me?"

"Just you," Aleeya confessed.

He looked down into her face, crouching over her, allowing his deep tenor to take a slight dip. "And what's so special about me that I have the pleasure of getting to know you're…less than shy side?"

Looking into his mesmerizing green eyes, she didn't care if he knew how she felt about him. This was their last day, and it would take a sheer miracle for her ever to see him again…so why not tell him? Why not say what was on her heart and let him deal with it? Lord knows how many men have said things to her and left without a trace.

"I'm showing you the person that you'll hopefully remember and miss when you get on the plane tomorrow and go off to live your life," she said, using her arms to elevate herself until her lips gently kissed the cleft within his chin. "I'm showing you the woman that made you laugh and at times made you shake your head in disbelief." She raised up again and kissed him on the cheek. "I'm showing you the woman that you have known for four short days but is blossoming because I'm in your presence."

Turing slowly on the board until she stood on her knees in front of him, Aleeya placed her arms around his waist of which Jenus responded by encircling her waist with his arms to keep them both steady.

"Finally, I'm showing you the woman who is going to miss you something terribly tomorrow." Her voice broke with the confession as tears fell down her cheeks.

He gently wiped the tears away with his thumb, then before she could say another word, his mouth found hers.

Too caught up to reason about where they were or what they were doing. Aleeya's body was awakening in response to his powerful embrace. It had been a long time that she had been held or felt special by the opposite sex. This was definitely not what she was aiming for when she came to Hawaii. Love wasn't something she had bargained for.

Besides, no one falls in love in three days. Aleeya had already bitten into too many rotten apples to believe in love at first sight. Still, her mom didn't raise a fool. So, she wasn't about to let a good man pass her by without savoring the moment.

She was just about to shimmy herself a little closer to his warmth when a nudge of the paddleboard caused them to abruptly shifted. Neither of them cared as they kept holding each other close. Then, another hard thump barreled into the paddleboard with such force, they both fell headfirst into the water. Right before she went under, she could've sworn she saw a gray fin heading straight toward them.

Later that evening...

"You made this day wonderful for me, Jenie... I'll never forget it!" she said, looking at their clasped hands as they slowly stopped in front of her hotel room. It really had been a wonderful day, and she had the pleasure of spending all of it with a great guy. Jenus had renewed her faith in believing in the kindness of others and that somewhere in the world where good guys still existed.

"You mean even the part where we got knocked off our paddleboard by dolphins?" He laughed, as did she.

"Yeah, even that, although that was pretty rotten of you not to let me know that you had taken me to Dolphin's Cove. I almost had a heart attack when I saw that gray fin coming at me."

"I had planned on telling you, but I guess I got a little distracted," he confessed, scratching his head.

"I guess we both did," she admitted while she blushed. "But don't worry, I have learned my lesson, and I am thankful that God didn't have to place me in the belly of a fish to learn it. Artie is safely tucked away for the evening. Level-headed sensible Aleeya is at the helm. Who is extremely grateful to God that I met you!"

"Also, I have placed Jenie in for the night. Only Jenus is here with you now." He picked the hand he was holding up and placed a lingering kiss on it. "Although, Aleeya, just like Artie, you have the most amazing brown eyes I have ever seen," he said in a whisper. Still, his eyes were focused on her lips.

"Really?" She cracked her door then stepped toward him placing her arms around his neck. "And does Jenie share your opinion with that?"

"Yes, we are both in agreement, to the point that if we ever lock eyes on them again, not even a shark will separate us." He let his nose dance with hers as their foreheads came together.

Aleeya's heartbeat became erratic as he moved closer to her face lowering his lips until they lightly brushed against hers.

"I believe I will miss your form of punishment most of all," he said right before his mouth found hers.

The kiss was so sweet and tender if she could have willed it, they'd stayed that way forever, but he broke the contact way too early. As their faces remained mere inches apart, their noses still wanting to do their own slow dance. Aleeya debated whether to let Artie out one more time and issue him some more mind-blowing punishment when a tingling sensation went off on her right hip.

There it was again…and again, this time a little stronger. As the realization set in, Aleeya began to giggle against his lips to his dismay.

"What in the world is so funny?" he said huskily, his eyebrows knitted together.

Aleeya's smiled up at him; her arms were still around his neck. Lightly she gave the tip of his nose a quick peck. "You're vibrating."

"What?"

"You're vibrating," she said, this time looking down toward the right side of his pants pocket. "Your phone."

"Oh!" Stepping back from her, and reached in his pocket to retrieve it, causing her to reluctantly give up her hold on him. Checking the number, he winced. "Oh, honey…I really need to take this. It's work," he said in an apologetic tone.

"It's all right, I understand... you're a wonderful man, Jenus Ballard. I'll never forget you." With that, admission she kissed him softly on the lips, stepped back into her room, and disappeared inside.

Chapter Ten

"A person's heart plans his way, but the Lord determines his steps". Proverbs 16:9 CSB

"Okay, spill it. What's on your mind, man?" Othniel asked as he worked his car into the heavy traffic away from the airport where he, Ascah, and Jenus just got in from the Hawaii conference.

Jenus remained quiet for a moment, just staring out the window at everything and then again nothing at all before answering. "Ben was acting strange, don't you think? I mean, why didn't he fly out with the rest of us?"

"Ben is acting no stranger than usual. I would say you're the one acting out of character," Othniel said while veering onto the freeway that would lead them to the interstate back toward their home in Indiana.

"He's up to something, I know it," Jenus said while fishing his sunglasses out of his front shirt pocket and placing them on his face. "He seems like he's planning something."

"You're the one to talk. And where exactly did you go yesterday? I thought we were all going to hang out, and you no-showed us.... again," Ascah pried. "You act as if you had some Hawaiian Holla girl stashed away somewhere."

"There you go with that overactive imagination of yours," Jenus countered.

"Well, it wasn't my imagination, neither was it Neil or Ben's, when we saw you slow dancing with some dark-haired beauty the second day of the trip. As a matter of fact, it looked like the same woman you were slow...slow dancing with last night...I have the pictures to prove it," she whispered in his ear.

"Ace, what did I tell you last night?" Othniel gave his wife a warning glare in the rearview mirror.

"That you liked my blue nightie best when it's crumpled on the floor," she said with a smirk.

"Ace!" Othniel yelled as the car swerved.

Jenus shut his eyes and rubbed his forehead, wishing he had thought to bring his own ride. Acsah was like a dog with a bone. Once she got hold of something, she wouldn't let it go.

"What!? You did say that." She batted her eyes innocently at her husband.

"You know what I'm talking about."

"Okay, fine Othniel," She rolled her eyes and pouted. "You're such a killjoy. Good Lord, Neil, we haven't been back home more than two minutes, and you're already fussing at me."

"That's because you have no filters."

"I do too. Just because they aren't as tightly screwed in as yours doesn't mean I don't have them."

"You know what, I'm not doing this with you right now." Othniel stated.

"Good, because I was talking to Jenus anyway. Now, as I was saying, Jenus, before being so rudely interrupted, what is the nature of your relationship with...oh I'm sorry, what's her name again?"

"Her name is None-ya," Jenus exclaimed.

"None-ya what? And you better not say business." She pointed at him as both men laughed. "Look, all I'm trying to do is get you hitched so I can have a new best friend at Indiana's campsite. You know, there're hardly any women at that campsite at all.

"We know, Ace, you've told me that over a hundred times," Othniel replied.

"Well, then I'm telling you for the one hundredth and one time. There are no women in Indiana, yet you insist on having me stay in a dry place. I don't understand why you haven't spoken to daddy and asked him for a reassignment."

"Acsah!" Othniel growled.

"You know what...fine. Neil, have it your way. Jenus, you can stay a bachelor until you nine hundred and fifty-two for all I care. And Neil, we can stay in that dry ole piece of land until those dry crumbled rocks crumble some more, see if I care. As a matter of fact, I'm not going to say a blessed word to either one of you until we get home." Acsah finished jerking sideways in her seat, cranked her music up, inserted her earbuds, then closed her eyes on the men seated in front.

Othniel looked at her in the rearview mirror. Seeing her eyes were shut, he looked at Jenus and mouthed the words thank God!

Jenus laughed to himself. He knew Neil loved Ace with all his heart, but she was definitely a handful, and that was putting things lightly. God had a way of bringing the two most unlikely people together. Neil was ultra-conservative while Acsah was ultra-crazy, but somehow, they seemed to balance each other out.

Balance. His mind immediately went to his time with Artie on the paddleboard. His heart started beating faster just thinking about her beautiful brown eyes. He sighed heavily. He missed her already, from her feistiness to the way she held on to him as they slow danced. And the punishment, Lord only knew how many cold showers and dips in the ocean he had to do just to keep his thoughts pure.

He wanted to spend every waking minute with her. Somehow being with her made missing his fiancée Nyla a little more bearable. Unfortunately, leaving paradise and the woman he had become quite attached to was now at an end. He was heading back to his real world and dealing with the routine stressors that came with being a director of a treatment facility for troubled kids.

He was ready to come back and face the new challenges, he was sure Ben and his brilliant ideas had conjured up for him and his staff this year. Yet, he also wanted something else. He hadn't thought about having a wife and family in seven years. But, after meeting Aleeya, a small beacon of hope began to ignite in his heart. It was strange and scary but also wonderful and stirring. Looking up in the sky, it comforted him knowing somewhere in the country, Aleeya was out there. He only prayed every now and then she would be thinking of him because God knows he'd be thinking about her.

"Earth to Jenus?" Othniel repeated.

So, caught up in his own thought, he hadn't even realized Neil was speaking to him. "Oh man, I'm sorry. What were you saying?"

"I was wondering what you thought of going back to Jericho? Are you okay with moving back? I know how relieved you were to get out of there and be someplace new?"

"Yeah...working with the Indiana group has been a breath of fresh air for the last two years. But with my parents getting older, and all this stuff going on with my sibs Rahab and Jess, I don't know; I guess going back is not so bad.

"You left out someone, didn't you?" Othniel pried.

Jenus gave a big sigh before speaking about his kid sister Raylin. "I'm trying to give my baby sister a little space."

"Well, you are better than me. If I thought for one moment that Jake the snake was on my sister's heels, I'd pound him." Othniel snarled.

"Oh, so I see how this works," Acsah spoke up. "I can't talk about Jenus' love life in front of him, but it's okay for you two to gossip about Raylin's love life behind her back."

"I thought you said you weren't going to say another blessed word," Othniel said, looking at his wife in the rearview mirror.

"I didn't say a blessed word. That was an entire statement of which I'm right." She sucked her teeth at her husband, who rolled his eyes in return.

"Anyway, as I said, you're a better man than me." Othniel commented as he switched lanes.

"Raylin doesn't need me prying or spying in her love life. Besides, Jake and I had a long talk about how I expect him to treat my sister. He knows it's not wise for him to cross the line," Jenus said, looking out the window, totally missing the look Othniel gave his wife.

"Well, maybe it is a good thing for you to go home and catch up on everything happening at Jericho," Othniel remarked in a clipped tone.

"Why'd you say it like that?" Jenus quickly turned to his friend. Something was up, and he knew it, and apparently, Othniel had caught wind of it too.

Othniel said with a shrug of his shoulders. "I didn't say it any special way."

Knowing he wouldn't get anywhere with Neil; he turned his attention to Acsah seated in the back. "So, Ace, what is Neil not telling me?"

"According to my husband, I'm not allowed to say one blessed word," Acsah said, still looking at her magazine.

"Look, I'd appreciate it if you guys would let me know what's going on so I don't get blindsided when I get to Jericho. Ben has been busy. I can tell by the way the board was acting the other day... something is up. Jake just called me last week, stating he was told that Ben was to handle all of the recruitment from now on. When I called Ben about it, he said it was the board's decision.   He claimed the board wanted to help Jake out since I was tied up with the expansion project," Jenus said mockingly, clearly agitated. "So, then I asked him about who all was currently registered and how many kids would be attending camp this year. All I was told was there would be fifty-five campers, of which twenty-five are female, and thirty are returning campers."

"So, you guys have a full house this year. Sounds great to me!" Acsah chimed in.

"Yeah, but the problem is we have room for fifty, and the girls' quarters hold eighteen beds."

"Oh...that could pose a problem," Othniel said solemnly.

"You think?"

"So, what did Ben say when you told him the camp was overbooked?"

"He said most of the time, some kids will likely drop out as the time to open the doors approaches. Then he said I worried too much and threw a scripture at me, saying all things work together for good," Jenus gripped. He knew he shouldn't be so critical. But ever since Ben was given ECA's liaison's position at the board's insistence, he and Jenus had been butting heads regularly. Ben had finesse and charm—he'd give him that. Especially when it came to rubbing elbows with those who had the financial means to support the academy's mission for the inner-city youth. But in his opinion, Ben was always the negotiator and wouldn't hesitate to finagle things to his advantage. It was the one quality that Ben possessed that bugged Jenus to no end.

"Well, he does have a point," Othniel interjected.

At Othniel's side comment, Jenus jerked his head toward his friend giving him an ominous glare.

"I'm sorry, did I miss something? When did *you* become Ben Rawlins's number one fan?"

"Don't go ballistic on me, man. All I'm saying is this could really be a good move for our cause. The more people know about what we're doing, the better. This could really steer the Eagle Crest in the right direction…."

"Oh, I didn't realize *you* thought we were headed in the wrong direction, Neil," Jenus said tersely.

"Oh, come on, Jenie, don't get all defensive. Ben can do some bizarre things, but his heart is in the right place. He is trying his best to bring outside attention to our cause which means more significant support and resources that could really benefit these kids," Acsah added.

"Et Brutis? So now the ECA is going down the wrong road?"

"Ballard, you need to chill," Othniel said, his voice beginning to rise a notch. "Where is all this hostility really coming from? You know I believe we're going in the right direction, and having extra funding to support what we're trying to accomplish only makes things better for the ECA's mission."

Jenus rubbed his eyes tiredly. He didn't know why he was so edgy today, but he didn't need to take it out on his friends. "Hey guys, I'm sorry. I guess I'm part tired and partly fed up with the way things are just being rapidly fired at us. These new changes the board and Ben have been throwing at me have just set me on edge, I guess. I want the camp to succeed and increase our revenue base, and at the last meeting, we came to an impasse on the new clientele they want brought to the ECA. I thought we had decided that things were going to remain the same this year, but apparently, *they* are moving forward," Jenus said with a deep sigh.

"I think with the expansion we're proposing in the next six months, we need to explore and consider the board's take on this Jenus," Othniel said in earnest. "If the ECA projects are going to meet the needs of the at-risk youth population, we better make sure we can deliver what we say. We need to know that the ECA program is duplicate-able and will work for the youth in New Haven and Millsboro, which are both much larger cities than Jericho."

"Exactly!" Acsah chimed in again. "How can we expect the same type of success if we don't allow kids with similar needs to come to the ECA so we can see if what we're doing works or needs to be tweaked?"

Jenus could feel his agitation on the rise again. He could tell Othniel, and his wife had sided with the board on this issue. Like the board, Ben didn't understand what that would mean for the people running the camp, mainly him. It was easy for them to think up stuff to implement because they weren't saddled with the burden of making it happen...he was.

"Neil and Ace, I hear you, and as I said before, I agree that this should *eventually* be an avenue we as an organization explore *slowly*. Give ourselves time to figure out how we want things to look and preparing our staff so we won't be going into this blind."

"And how long do we wait? Another three months, or six or eight...maybe we should think about another two years; that way, we can let the target population we want to serve slip right through our fingers. The harvest is plentiful *now*, Jenus, and they are staring us in the face right here and right now. We need to strike while the iron is hot," Othniel said with urgency.

"But at what price, having a camp full of rambunctious youth we can't handle?" Jenus quickly interjected. "Look, I'm all for looking toward the ECA's future but are we prepared to take on the needs of *these kids* and their families?"

Rubbing his hand over his chin, Othniel remained quiet for a moment." Yeah, I guess you have a point," Othniel said.

"Right now, we have a lot of youth involved in risky behaviors that are salvageable. But adding kids with dual diagnosis to the mix...." Jenus rolled his eyes while shaking his head. "Man, we're asking for trouble."

Except for Ace humming to the music playing in the background, they drove in silence. Othniel's eyes were glued to the road. At the same time, Jenus looked out the passenger's window, deep in thought about Aleeya Thomas and his desire to see her again. Remembering she had texted him, he grabbed his phone and read her message.

"Jenus, I know we promised to conclude our relationship once we came back to the mainland...But honestly, I just can't get you out of my mind. I miss your smile, your laughter but more than anything, how perfectly delicious it felt to be held in your arms. Is it normal to feel this way after so short of time knowing each other? I don't know, but I felt this strange comfort being in your presence. I guess I was wondering if you felt it too. Anyway, I couldn't tell you last night, but you helped me reconnect with my adventurous side. I had it buried inside me for so long, I forgot what it felt like to step out and take a risk. In this short stay in Hawaii, God used you to remind me that life is better when you take a few risks every now and then. So, thank you for everything, and I just want you to know that I'll be thinking of you often on my journey home. PS. I would say that you were my part-time guardian angel this week, but the way you kiss.... Umm...honey, you're definitely no angel (smiley face). If I ever see you again...just know paradise was a little sweeter for me...because you were there. Missing you, Artie!"

He closed the text and sighed deeply. *Artie felt it too,* he thought inwardly. There was this strange vibe, a connection between them he couldn't explain but wanted to explore. He wasn't one for a long-distance relationship; they usually didn't work for him. But there was no way on earth he would not explore this thing brewing between them. It was impossible to explain what he was thinking and feeling in a text. So Jenus pocketed his phone, deciding to have a long conversation with her as soon as he was alone.

Chapter Eleven

"The Lord is my light and my salvation of whom shall, I fear?   The Lord is the strength of my life; of whom shall I be afraid?" Psalms 27:1

Muffled voices danced in Aleeya head. Shouts, screams, sirens, all fused to make an impenetrable wall of noise. Then Terry Kincaid's voice with his filthy contemptuous words blared in her head. *"You good for nothing, interfering whore!"* The insult hurt just as much as his kick to her ribs. Then there was nothing…no pain, no noise…nothing. Total silence and peace like a tranquil river flowed over her. She sighed and took a breath, relieved she was away from that awful person. Opening her eyes, to her delight, she saw her mother's smiling face looked down on her like she had when she was a little girl waking from a nightmare.

Faithfully her mother was always there. Aleeya smiled and was ready to drift off to sleep and would've, but her mother was saying something.

"I can't hear you. Mom, what did you say?" Aleeya strained to hear Betty over what sounded like rushing water.   Squinting to see her mom, who was now standing in front of a beautiful waterfall.   As her mother's form began to fade behind the thickening cloud of mist, Aleeya spoke louder.   "Mom, what are you saying?"

Giving her daughter the sweetest smile, Betty repeated herself. This time Aleeya could hear her clearly.

"Artie, it's time for you to return home to Jericho!"

"What?" Aleeya frowned, trying to understanding.

"Artie, it's time to go back home."

Looking again where her mother stood, the sound of the rushing waterfall still emanating its distinct sound, but her mother had disappeared through its white mist. The only thing left was her repetitive words. It's time to go home. Realization began setting in. Popping open her eyes, Aleeya stared at an unfamiliar ceiling as her cell phone kept chiming its annoying tune. Impulsively she grabbed her pillow, ready to throw it at the offending sound, but instead stilled her hand and closed her eyes again in the hope of seeing one more glimpse of her mother's smiling face. It was to no avail. Her mother's happy face was gone like the night. It was time...it was time for her to return home to Jericho.

Immediately Terry's face popped into her mind.

"INTERFERING WHORE!"

Aleeya shut her eyes tight and began to boldly declare, "I am fearfully and wonderfully made. I am a royal priesthood and a holy nation!" Aleeya kept quoting scriptures decreeing who she was in Christ until Terry's face and his nasty words faded. Peace like a tranquil river flowed over her. Sighing, she finished quoting the twenty-seventh Psalm, then said an additional prayer to cover the day, kicking the covers off, she ran to the bathroom to shower and dress. "Lord, I'm running so late. I'll be lucky if I can get a cup of coffee at Starbucks," she fussed.

Twenty minutes later, she came out of the bathroom freshly scrubbed and moved toward her closet to look for a comfortable outfit. This was her last day in paradise, and she wasn't going to waste it. All night she had hoped and prayed Jenus would respond to her text, but he hadn't. Grabbing her favorite maxi dress, she turned to the mirror to see it up against her.

"Lord, I thought he was different. It sure felt like he was different from the rest. Just goes to show you, everything that looks good might not be suitable for you." She sighed, wrinkling up her nose at the dress she was considering. After all, today was a special day. She smiled, turning her attention to the dresser that held the small urn.

"I can't believe this is the last place on our list," Aleeya spoke out in the quietness of her room, choking back a sudden wave of emotion. Moving toward the dresser and picking up the box, she headed toward the balcony to view the sun rising in the morning sky. She smiled, feeling her mom's presence in the room.

"Honey, you think this is paradise? Just wait until you get to heaven."

Aleeya inhaled the ocean air deeply and allowed the remainder of the troubling dream to flow out of her. "I've had a wonderful time traveling from place to place, leaving a bit of you everywhere we visited. I just wish…." Aleeya bowed her head, allowing the tears she could no longer hold to fall.

"Lelee. I know you miss me, but it was my time. I've proudly served the Lord, and being in His continual presence is my reward. I'm already dead to this world, and now my life is in Christ for all eternity. As much as I love you, I would never trade heaven to come back to this ole world, not for a second. When we live on earth, we don't think there is anything but this life. We talk about heaven like it's a fantasy world, but honey, it's real. You know that song I like to sing…I traded my old tatter garment, and he gave me a robe of pure white. I'm feasting on manna from heaven…that's why I'm happy tonight. That's the reality I live now."

Aleeya's heart warmed as she heard the song verse play over and over in her mom's strong alto. She found herself singing along, remembering the many days they sang together in the house just praising God. She sorely missed those days.

"Now listen, Lelee, there you go getting all sentimental on me. Look, you have carried around dead things far too long. It's time for you to go on with your life and start living."

"Mom…it's so hard." Her voice wobbled.

"Baby life being hard ain't nothing new. Always remember God's word has the final say, and in his word, Jesus commands for you to be of good cheer because he has overcome this ole world, and that means so can you," Betty reminded her.

Aleeya bowed her head. She knew her mother's words were spot on. But coming out of her comfortable cocoon after five years of solitude, she wasn't sure if she was ready to reenter the world she left behind. But before she could voice that thought, her mom spoke up again.

"Honey their ain't no way God put his word in you, gave you that fancy education and brilliant mind, for you to waste it. He wants you to help others, not going from one side of the country to the other spreading my remains. He's called you to spread the gospel, not ashes."

"I know what your saying is right. I never thought at thirty-five, I'd still be doing things…alone, though."

"Girl, you are never alone. Jesus goes before you, the angles keep watch over you, and the Holy Spirit is inside you. What else do you need?"

Her mind immediately went to Jenus. No, he hadn't called like she hoped he would. Maybe he was just a figment of her imagination like her mother was. But he sure didn't kiss like one. She smiled to herself as she bit her nails. Turning slightly, she saw her mother staring at her with a smirk on her face as she just shook her head.

"You and those hormones." Her mother chuckled. "You may not believe this, but honey, God knows all about your lonely heart and those raging desires. But no matter how bad you think you need a man; God's timing is perfect. The husband you want, when you get your focus right, you'll run smack dab into him. Just wait and see."

How she ran into Jenus immediately popped up in her mind, but she quickly squashed it. If he was interested, he would have at least responded to her text, wouldn't he?

"Girl, if you don't get your eyes off that boy and get yourself together. Daylight is burning, and you're wasting it with your head stuck in the clouds."

Aleeya shook herself, heeding her mother's warning. Jenus was nothing more than a junior high crush from an eighth grader's hormones. It was nice to see someone from back home, but he was gone; time to put the fantasy away. Moving to the closet, she grabbed a pair of jean capris and a white shirt and quickly put them on. Sliding her feet into her flip-flops, she then went over and picked up her mom's remains. "So, Mom, where are we going first? She spoke to the silence in the room.

"I already showed you. I want my last remains to be caught up amid the mist from the waterfall."

"Okay, Mom…Dolphin Cove it is," Aleeya said picking up the small alabaster-colored box, then gathered her keys, and purse. With mother's urn in hand, she made her way out the door, just as the sun was breaking over the clouds. Today was going to be a glorious yet bittersweet day.

Chapter Twelve

"In the world you shall have distress; but have confidence, I have overcome the world." John 16:33 DRB

It was finished. Aleeya sat on her balcony with her feet propped up, sipping on her ice tea while enjoying the beautiful sunset. The reddening fireball cast its setting rays on the clouds turning the sky shades of purple and gold. Indeed, it was a sight to behold. The best the earth had to offer. Still, it was nothing in comparison to the majestic beauty her mother must be experiencing in heaven. A warm breeze crossed her face bring both a smile and tears with the thought of her mother being in her eternal paradise with those she loved so dear. Closing her eyes, she could still hear her mother's voice giving her, as she called it, her farewell speech.

"You can't hide from life…Lelee. You have to live it. In this life, the Word of God says you would have trouble, you would have tribulations, but be of good cheer because our Savior has overcome this world. So, stop hiding from life. Live…take a few risks and when you're afraid of something…do it anyway. Remember whose backing you up."

With that, she watched as her mother faded into the mist coming off the waterfall. As the spray shot up in the air and disappeared, so did her mother's face, transcending with a smile that was brighter than the midday sun. Those around her were never the wiser, even when tears streamed down her face in the wonder of the glorious sight the Lord let her see. She still heard her mother's parting words while having lunch at the little café she and Jenus frequented. Aleeya was pondering just how to take the brakes off and live a little when the phone rang with Ben's solid tenor on the other end.

"Hey there."

"Hey there yourself." She cleared her throat, curious of the sudden goosebumps appearing on her arms at the sound of his voice.

"Are you still enjoying yourself in paradise?"

"Yeah, although it's boring now that the conference is over and just about everyone has left.

"Oh, so you've been left without a dance partner, huh?"

Aleeya scrunched up her face at the phone, wondering where that comment came from, but before she could ask, he spoke up.

"Listen, I have a proposal for you."

"Well, that's not romantic at all. Proposing over the phone, no wonder you're not hitched yet." She laughed, knowing his long pause meant he hadn't got her joke. Then his laughter broke through loud and clear.

"You know what, Artie McFartie, you better quit clowning on me, or I'll revoke the offer that I haven't even offered yet."

"Yeah...yeah...yeah." She waved off the threat. "Now, what can I do for you, Benjamin?" She enunciated his first name, knowing he'd hate it.

"First, you can never call me Benjamin like that again." He chuckled.

"Well, I had to get you back for that Artie McFartie, which I believe you were the one who told the entire high school it was my nickname."

"I swear I didn't. I just told one person." He continued laughing.

"Who...who did you tell?" she pressed while thinking that laughter was indeed medicine for the soul.

"Mark Warner."

"Mark Warner!" Aleeya's eyes went wide. She quickly covered her mouth as she realized she had said her classmate's name rather loud, gathering some stares from other patrons. "I used to have the biggest crush on him. I think once I got through that gawky stage with the braces and acne...he might have asked me out."

"Yeah, I know, and there were quite a few other things he would have asked of you. So, I told him a few things."

"Ben, you didn't!" She doubled over in laughter. Mark Warner was the biggest player in school and not because of his skills on the basketball court. That dude went after girls like a hummingbird went after nectar. Ben's little act of interference probably spared her several bouts of VD, among other things. After a few more laughs, she settled herself down. "My good sir, your sense of chivalry will not go unrewarded, so I guess I owe you big time, so what is this non-marriage proposal about?"

"Well, like I told you. Eagles Crest Academy aims to transform its entire program into a more therapeutic entity in the residential community. After submitting your program, the board has approved it with a few minor adjustments. But the one major condition is you have to come and personally implement the program."

Her mouth hung open for several seconds as a montage of thoughts bombarded her mind. This was really happening. The program she had developed in grad school was going to receive the breath of life.

"Yeah, but it's in Jericho." A dark thought screamed.

Aleeya could hear the voice of her fears speaking so loudly she turned around to make sure it wasn't an actual person speaking behind her.

"Aleeya…are you still there?"

Ben's voice broke in on the tirade of fear speaking to her mind. Then her mother's words came back to her.

"You've got to take some risks. Think of all the things that you'll possibly miss because you're too afraid to take a step of faith. For the last five years, you've been going around trying to get your life together. You've been doing everything right being

very conscious of everything that you do just so you can avoid trouble. But honey, that's not living. That's not the life God intended for you to have. You have to understand that everything you face every situation that seems too big for you. It's not too big for God. You've got to trust Him and know he has your back."

Her mother was right. It was time to step out on faith and believe God had her. "Yes, and yes."

"Meaning?"

"Yes, I'm still here, and yes, I will take the position," Aleeya said, sitting up a little straighter to keep her knees from shaking. Although her traitorous body didn't seem to agree with her decision, she sounded sure of herself.

"Even though that means moving home to Jericho?" he said with hesitation.

"Well, that's where the offer is, so that's where I plan to be." The burrito she was eating for lunch went sour in her stomach. Pushing the plate of food away, she resolved it in her mind that she wasn't going to let fear shove her around anymore.

"Humph."

Humph? Aleeya thought that was an odd way for Ben to express his gratitude for her accepting his offer. "After I told you I'd come and bring this glorious revitalization to the ECA, all you can say is humph?"

"No, that's not it. I'm thrilled about you coming home. I just thought I had to do more convincing. I had a whole speech planned and everything. I was even going to consider enticing you with a possible marriage proposal if I thought it would've gotten me somewhere. Then you up and accepted the offer just like that."

"Well, I'm in a generous mood."

"Yes, I can see that." He paused a little while before speaking again. "It almost makes me wish I would have come at you with the marriage proposal first." He chuckled.

"You would be so lucky." Aleeya flirted.

"No, you're lucky we have a no fraternization policy in place at the ECA…or you might have your hands full when you reach the academy."

"Aw, so you're playing the hero again, Mr. Rawlins, trying to save me from something."

"Perhaps…but if you play your cards right, I have some pull with the board and might just have the policy rescinded."

"Again, you would be so lucky." She jested, but somehow, she had a feeling there was a little more to the conversation than he was letting on, but she wouldn't press it. She had made a choice, and felt it was a good one. What would welcome her once she reached Jericho? Only time would tell.

Chapter Thirteen

"For Adonai Elohim will help. This is why no insult can wound me. This is why I have set my face like flint, knowing I will not be put to shame." Isaiah 50:7 CJB

On her last morning in paradise, God was even more gracious to Aleeya by displaying a beautiful sunrise. It was full of brilliant hues of oranges mixed in with deep reds filling the morning sky with a host of vivid colors. Nestled in her hotel robe, she stood in her doorway thinking of all that transpired that day and, for that matter, the entire week. The loud ring of her hotel telephone startled her out of her thoughts and back into the present. Pulling her feet off the balcony rail, she hurried into the room and plopped on the bed before it went to the third ring. "Hello."

"Hey, brown eyes…I've missed you." Jenus deep tenor rumbled over the receiver.

She quickly covered the mouthpiece of her phone, so he couldn't hear her squeal with glee. After the text she sent him last night and him not responding, she had thought that it meant he just wasn't that into her. "Lord, thank you, and I take back all the stuff I said about men." She inwardly prayed.

"Hi there," she said, still a little stunned at his call. Then she quickly added, "I've missed you too. Hawaii is a little less like paradise now that you're not here." She immediately rolled her eyes, slapped her forehead, and fell back on the bed, amazed at how corny she sounded.

"So, you're saying I've made a memorable impression on you?"

"Yes, although I wish I could say I had the same impact on you," She countered, just a tad bit miffed that he never responded to her text.

"On the contrary, Ms. Thomas. When I saw your text, we were on our way home. I was going to call you as soon as we made a stop, but, well, I kinda had a little accident with the phone."

"Oh really...what kind of an accident?" she questioned.

"The kind where you absently place the phone on the hood of the car, then drive off."

"Oh...I see." She covered the receiver so he wouldn't hear her giggling.

"Yeah, so it took a minute to get it replaced."

Her heart melted. "Well, in that case, I repent for the mean things I was thinking about you."

"Oh really, care to share?"

"Well, let's just say I was placing you in a category that you definitely don't belong in...for that, I am sorry, and we'll leave it at that." Aleeya bit her bottom lip wishing she hadn't divulged even that. Paul had put her through so much drama before he left her for good. She had spent two weeks in the hospital, mending after her attack. During that entire time, Aleeya was calling and texting Paul, but he never responded. She didn't know if he was alive or dead until she came home to a stack of bills, his room emptied along with a lot of her furniture. The only thing he hadn't taken was his share of the rent... the louse.

"Humph, so I miss one text, and I'm already assigned a category, and from the way you sound, that's not a good category to be in."

"I think you forget that I repented, and I said I was sorry," she reminded.

"I don't know, Ms. Thomas, its sure sounds to me like you deserve some of that punishment you seemed so eager to dish out to me while we were together." His voice dropped an octave lower.

"Yeah, too bad you're not here, I love to give you some of that punishment." She sighed, wishing there wasn't an ocean separating them. "I guess I'll owe you."

"Or, in a couple of months, I can just come down to Florida for a little rest and punishment then," he suggested with a chuckle.

Aleeya scrunched her face up. She had already contacted her university and set herself up to teach online classes. Once she returned from this trip, she planned on packing up and driving back home to Jericho. Maybe now was a good time for her to come out with her little secret. Taking a deep, cleansing breath, she spoke. "About that, although I would love for you to come and see me in Florida, I won't be there."

"Why?"

"Well, I got a new job, so I'm moving back to my hometown next month."

"Oh…well, I still can come to see you unless your hometown doesn't have roads or an airport." He jested.

"Well, the closest airport is the Pittsburgh International Airport, and even then, you would likely have to drive nearly three hours to see me…in Jericho."

There was a long moment of silence on Jenus's end. It was just long enough to make a person feel uncomfortable but not long enough to start babbling hysterically about anything that came to mind. Unable to take it a second longer Aleeya opened her mouth to speak when she heard Jenus deep chuckle on the other end.

"This new job opportunity wouldn't happen to be at Eagle Crest Academy, would it?"

Aleeya sat up on the bed a little straighter, puzzled. "Well yeah, but how did you know?"

"Did a Mr. Ben Rawlins offer this position to you?"

"Yes?" Aleeya said hesitantly, feeling a little uneasy. "I mean, he hired me, but he's not going to be my boss from what I'm told. That position hasn't been filled yet."

"Actually, that's inaccurate. The position has been filled."

Her heart began racing, but she didn't understand why. "Okay, Jenus, wait a minute. Why do you know so much about this? I only spoke with Ben yesterday about taking the position."

"Yes, and I just confirmed with him and the board that I would also be taking a position there too."

"Really?" Her heart fluttered. They would be co-workers and hopefully much more. It was a dream come true. "What's your position?" She asked, curious but also noticing a shift in his tone.

"I'll be your boss," he said flatly.

It was her turn to remain silent. Jenus was going to be her boss! She couldn't even begin to wrap her head around that. To say things would be a little awkward at the academy was an understatement. Then she remembered the no fraternization policy Ben had mentioned. Seeing how they had already put the cart before the horse in that area, it would be a challenge to right things now. Realizing neither one of them had said anything for a while, she broke the silence between them. "Well, I got to say, this wasn't the way I saw our conversation going." She nervously chuckled. "I guess we'll need to rethink that whole punishment thing." Aleeya closed her eyes, wishing she could drop through the floor.

"Oh…I don't know. I think I like our current arrangement. I think we should keep it in play."

"But Ben said there was a no fraternization policy at the camp?"

"How do you know Ben, anyway?"

Noticing how he completely dismissed her concerns about the policy, she explained how she knew Ben. "Well, we all went to Jericho High School. Well, I wasn't in the same grade as Ben. He was a year ahead of me. As a matter of fact, you and I…um…" Aleeya abruptly stopped herself before she repeated the embarrassing way they had first met. "Umm anyway, Ben was a year ahead of me, so we were in some of the same clubs."

"Don't tell me Ben is an ex-boyfriend of yours?"

"No…no, not at all, he's just a friend," she said, a little irritated that he was giving her the third degree. "You do know that men and women can be friends without strings, don't you?"

"I don't know. I'm thinking about our paddleboard outing. It didn't seem as if we did a good job at managing the whole without strings thing!"

"I-I…um." Aleeya cleared her throat, utterly flustered at his honesty. "Well, I plan on keeping a tight rein on Artie's strings from here on in so you don't have to worry about that." She assured.

"Oh, I wasn't worried about that. It's just that I'm the type of boss who is a stickler for following the rules, but I don't know how I'm going to manage that with you underfoot at the campsite." He paused, then spoke up again. This time his voice softened with his words. "Although I've heard it said rules are made to be broken from time to time, and I plan on break quite a few of them with you."

The tension in her shoulders drained away at his confession. Laying back on her bed, she wished she could caress his face like she did the last time they kissed. "Well, Mr. Ballard, I too am a stickler for the rules. I can assure you, for every rule you break, I personally plan on doling out the most delightful punishments equal to your offenses."

"Artie, darling, I'm looking forward to it, and by the way, welcome to Eagle Crest Academy and welcome home to Jericho."

Aleeya had hung up with Jenus two hours ago and was still smiling. He had promised to keep in touch as she transition back east. She was so down with that and told him she'd make sure he'd receive more than one punishment just to make the trip worthwhile.

"The trip would be worth it even if it was just one."

With those words in mind, she packed up the rest of her things and placed her suitcases at the door. She was all set to leave paradise and embark on the journey ahead of her. Settling herself on the bed until it was time to check out, Aleeya allowed her mind to drift to Jenus's other declaration, *Welcome home to Jericho.*

After all the trauma and drama, she went through five years ago, Aleeya never thought she'd call Jericho home again. Yet here she was planning to move back there. At least God had made the deal sweet by throwing Jenus Ballard in the mix but still. "God, it would be nice to know what I'm supposed to do when I get there she said in a silent prayer.

"Take The City!"

It was just a whisper, but it resounded so loud in her spirit that she couldn't help but sit up in bed and hold on to herself. She wasn't a stranger to God's voice, and it was clear that he was speaking to her now.

"Take the city!" Aleeya repeated the words she just heard inwardly. She had no idea what they meant. Only God knew for now. Laying back down, she quietly prayed to God.

"Lord, I don't understand why you've called me to return to Jericho, but I'm willing to follow your lead. Guide my way and make every crooked path straight. And I thank you in advance for going before me in Jesus's name…Amen!" With the prayer said, Aleeya looked at the ceiling and boldly declared,

"Ready or not Jericho, here I come!"

God Encounter

Like Aleeya and Jenus, sometimes God requires us to revisit situations, places, and even people that have caused us to get stuck on this journey called life. But trusting God enough to go back is not always easy. Dealing with our past pain, uncertain futures, and encountering a different aspect of God can be overwhelming. This is what Aleeya was experiencing…and maybe you are too.

Aleeya didn't want to return to her hometown in Jericho because of the past still haunting her. She thought she had put the past behind her. However, the notion of going back caused the past with the old hurts to resurface. Making her struggle to accept God's plan for her future.

- In what areas in your life can you identify with Aleeya when it comes to revisiting areas of your past?
  - What do you need in order to be whole in this area?
    - Do you need forgiveness?
    - Do you need to forgive others?
    - Do you need to be healed emotionally?
- Aleeya struggled with keeping the past in the past. Can you relate to this struggle? How so?

- Philippians 3:13-14 tells us to forget those things behind us and press towards those things ahead of us. In what ways did Aleeya do this? In what creative ways can you push forward and leave your past issues behind?
- Aleeya had a plan that didn't come to pass, causing her to get stuck. When things you desire don't happen, how do you respond? Do you find yourself getting stuck in what didn't happen?
- Sometimes we think we have God all figured out. However, when he redirects our plans or doesn't do what we thought he was going to do, it throws us for a loop. In what areas has God been trying to teach you something new about His ways?
  - What old thoughts or beliefs do you have to let go of to understand how God is trying to reveal himself to you now?

Let's Pray:

Heavenly Father, I pray for every reader. I pray that you give grace to those struggling to get unstuck while on their journey. I pray the peace from the Holy Spirit's presence covers them as you navigate them towards their destination. I pray that their faith in you never fails and that they continue to trust you as you get them safely to the other side, in Jesus' name.... Amen!

Note from the Author

I hope you enjoyed reading this story. Return to Jericho is loosely based on the biblical story about Jericho after the wall surrounding the city fell down (Joshua 6:1-27). Rahab and her family were the only survivors of Jericho after the town was conquered by Joshua and the Children of Israel. Although we don't know anything about Rahab's family or what happened to them afterwards, some biblical historians claim that Joshua eventually married Rahab.

Although there is not a biblical account of how the newly occupied city was rebirthed. We can assume that the city had to be constructed and established by someone while the men fought to conquer more territory. That reconstruction had to be accomplished by the women and older men left behind.

So often, women are not given credit for their contributions in the biblical story; however, if you look for them, they can be found. God uses ordinary people, both male, and female, to bring his will to pass. So never feel that God can't use you to do something extraordinary. Remember, you plus God make a majority.

Stay tuned for the next book in the Women of Jericho series entitled. *Follow My Lead* coming in 2022. While you're waiting, check out my other novels for purchase at Amazon.com:

Keturah the II
***Keturah II to* None**

I would love to hear from you. Please visit my website vicstories.com, or find me on Facebook at HerBet Publishing, on Instagram mosleyvicke, or email me at vicstories17@gmail.com.

Always remember, there is victory in your story.

Blessings, Vickie